She felt

Jim could barely believe he was holding Carrie in his arms. She was the softest thing he'd touched in years. Her lips were warm and she tasted of chocolate. Why had it taken him so long to kiss her, when he'd been aching to do just that since he'd first walked into her office?

Just then Carrie wrenched her mouth from his and tore herself away. Not even looking at him, she stammered, "I—I have to go." Then she ran across the patio toward the house.

Jim stood there dazed and suddenly bereft by the loss of the woman in his arms. For years he'd told himself he needed no one, but right now he realized how much he needed—how much he wanted—Carrie. And that could mean only one thing. Trouble.

Dear Reader,

I don't know about you, but as a little girl I fantasized about having an older brother. One who was bigger, older and wiser than me. In the CHILDREN OF TEXAS series, after writing about the three girls in the Barlow family, I'm finally writing about their big brother, James (Jim) Barlow. It's rather odd when your big brother is thirty-one when you first meet him, but the three girls have an immediate response to Jim, and he to them.

Maybe I write strong men who love their families because of my dad. He was strong, brave and a family man. He was even a hero, because he was a fireman. He spent his free time doing things with the four of us, even though only one of us was a boy, my younger brother. But Daddy taught us all to shoot a gun, catch fish and hike in the woods. Some might consider these "man" things, but Daddy didn't distinguish between us.

I hope you enjoy Jim's trials and tribulations and the family love that he finds. As they always say, you never can have too much family. Especially when you've been alone for a long time.

Happy reading!

Judy Christenberry

Judy Christenberry

A SOLDIER'S RETURN

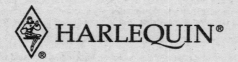

HARLEQUIN®

TORONTO • NEW YORK • LONDON
AMSTERDAM • PARIS • SYDNEY • HAMBURG
STOCKHOLM • ATHENS • TOKYO • MILAN • MADRID
PRAGUE • WARSAW • BUDAPEST • AUCKLAND

ISBN 0-373-75077-3

A SOLDIER'S RETURN

www.eHarlequin.com

Printed in U.S.A.

ABOUT THE AUTHOR

Judy Christenberry has been writing romances for over fifteen years because she loves happy endings as much as her readers do. A former French teacher, Judy now devotes herself to writing full-time. She hopes readers have as much fun with her stories as she does. She spends her spare time reading, watching her favorite sports teams and keeping track of her two daughters. Judy lives in Texas.

Books by Judy Christenberry

HARLEQUIN AMERICAN ROMANCE

*Brides for Brothers
†Tots for Texans
**Children of Texas

Prologue

Carrie Abrams was working on her computer when she heard the door of the detective agency open.

She turned her body to greet the entrant, but her eyes were still focused on completing the task on her computer screen. She clicked Save and reluctantly brought her eyes to the person standing by the door. Spit-shined shoes, crisp khaki pants, belted jacket...

As her gaze rose up the tall, straight-postured man before her, she saw he was a military man. A well-built military man. She looked at his face—and gasped.

"Jim!"

At the odd look on the man's face, she retracted the surprised greeting. "I—I mean— Sorry, I mistook you for someone I, um—" She was stammering like a blubbering fool, but she couldn't help it. That was a common result when one met one's fantasy-come-to-life. Grabbing hold of herself, she cleared her throat and said in her best professional voice, "May I help you?"

"I need to speak with Will Greenfield."

"And your name?" She almost held her breath.

"Captain James Barlow."

She knew it! She'd recognize that face anywhere. After all, she'd been staring at his picture for over a year. But the man was even better looking in person.

On rather unsteady feet she got up from her desk, suddenly wishing she'd worn something other than a pair of jeans and a bulky sweater. *You're being silly,* she told herself. Jim Barlow wouldn't care what she was wearing. He didn't even know her.

She rapped on Will's door and opened it at his say-so, then stepped inside, closed the door and leaned against it.

"He's here!" She whispered so the man in the outer office wouldn't hear her.

"Who—" Will started to ask, but Carrie didn't wait. "Jim! He's here. And he wants to see you."

Will's face broke into a smile. "Well, show him in!"

More than anything Carrie wanted to stay in Will's office, to be part of the discussion with the captain, but she knew she couldn't ask. It wouldn't be professional.

And it was Will's case, after all, not to mention part of his extended family.

Instead, she opened the door. "Captain Barlow, please come in." She leaned against the door, reluctant to break contact with the men. Then her gaze was caught by the warning glint of the silver frame on her desk. Right near where the man was standing.

"Oh, no!" She rushed forward. Jim's picture was on her desk. Had he seen it? She hoped not. How could she explain her fascination with Vanessa's oldest brother?

The explanation was simple really. In her work as a

private investigator for Greenfield and Associates, she found it easier to understand the person she was looking for if she had a photo of him or her. In this case, though, the picture hadn't prepared her for the fact that Jim Barlow was an absolute hunk. He was taller than she realized, with thick muscles that in person couldn't be hidden by his uniform. His dark hair didn't surprise her, since his three sisters had the same brown color, but his chocolate eyes glinted with golden highlights in the overhead light. Yes, he was a definite hunk!

They'd found Jim early on in their investigation, so that excuse for his picture didn't really work. It was just that. An excuse. The truth was she'd been fascinated by his square-jawed image ever since she'd first seen the standard-issue marine photograph. Vanessa had been, too. He was the picture of protective, strong…safe. The big brother every little girl dreamed of. The man every woman dreamed of.

Her best friend, Vanessa Shaw, had probably dreamed those dreams as she was raised as an only child. Then, after her father's death, her mother had told her that she was adopted and that she had five siblings. That revelation had set in motion a chain of events that had brought tremendous changes in their lives.

Carrie drew a deep breath. It was so tempting to call Vanessa and break the news. But she couldn't do that. That was Will's privilege.

All she could do was sit here and pretend indifference that Jim Barlow had returned to the bosom of his family after twenty-three years.

Chapter One

"Mr. Greenfield," Jim said crisply in greeting as the tall, middle-aged man came around his desk.

"Captain Barlow, welcome. May I call you Jim?"

Jim nodded. If he was right, Greenfield wasn't the only one who thought of him as Jim. The receptionist had said she'd mistaken him for someone else, but if that was true, it was quite a coincidence.

"Sit down, Jim. We didn't expect you for several more months."

"Yes, I made a decision to get out of the marines. I thought I'd come meet my sisters, unless this is an inconvenient time."

"Lord have mercy, you walk out of here without seeing them and my wife would divorce me, and those three young ladies would never speak to me again!"

"Your wife would divorce you?" Jim asked, a little surprised by Greenfield's response.

"Vanessa didn't tell you I married her mother?"

"No. In fact, she hasn't told me much of anything. Her letters have been filled with questions about me."

"Well, then, there's a lot we have to talk about." He reached for the phone. "But first I'll call the house and let them know you're here. Our housekeeper will want to make a welcome-home dinner. Then we can go over there, or I can answer any questions you have first."

Jim watched the man talk with someone named Betty.

"Yes, I'll tell her. I'm sure she'll accept. Tell Viv when she wakes up. And call Vanessa and Rebecca."

After he hung up the phone, the man looked at Jim. "My wife is still napping. Our son still gets us up several times a night."

Jim didn't want to ask any awkward questions, but he thought Greenfield was a bit old to have a baby son.

Will sighed. "I should've guessed they didn't tell you about our baby, either." He sat back in his chair and nodded at the photo on his desk. An attractive blonde held a blue-blanketed newborn.

"Vivian adopted Vanessa during her first marriage. She was married at eighteen. She's just turned forty-four." He shrugged a shoulder and grinned. "We didn't plan on another family, but we're thrilled about our son. He's five months old."

"Congratulations," Jim said, relieved to have things clarified.

"Do you have other questions before we go to the house?"

Jim drew a deep breath. He had so many questions, it'd take a lifetime to ask them. But before he could ask any, the phone rang again.

"Excuse me," Will said. After a minute, he covered the phone receiver and explained to Jim, "I'm sorry, but

I've got to take this call." He raised his voice and called out, "Carrie?"

The young woman appeared at the door. "Yes, Will?"

"Could you answer any questions Jim might have while I finish this call?"

"Of course. Come with me, Jim—I mean Captain Barlow."

"'Jim' will be fine," he said, rising and moving into the outer office again. "There's no need to entertain me. I'll go back to my hotel and call Will tomorrow."

"No!" she replied, grabbing his arm. "You can't leave!" Carrie felt his muscles tense under her hold, and she looked at him, noting an accompanying hardening of his features.

"Unless I'm under house arrest, I don't see any reason why I can't...Carrie, is it?"

She withdrew her hand from his arm. "I—I didn't mean I could stop you, Jim. I meant it would be a disappointment to your family if you left today without seeing any of them."

"I doubt that, Carrie. They haven't seen me since the twins were two. And Vanessa was three months old when she was adopted. She definitely doesn't remember me."

The only sibling he'd had contact with was Wally because they'd both gone in the foster-care system. Wally had followed him into the marines—and had been killed at twenty-eight.

He'd told his sisters, and Will, about his brother's death. He hadn't forgiven himself for Wally's end. After all, Wally had joined the marines only because Jim had.

He cleared his throat. "I'm sure waiting until tomorrow won't make any difference."

"Jim, I'm a friend of Vanessa's. I know how much she's been longing to see you. Please, just wait a few minutes. I'm sure Will won't be long."

With a sigh, Jim sat down in one of the chairs in front of her desk. "Will said he married Vanessa's mother."

"Yes, last spring, and they have a son, Danny."

"So the baby is Vanessa's brother?"

"Technically he's her half brother." She smiled. "It's quite a story, you know. Last year Vanessa only had her adoptive mother, Vivian. Now she has a stepfather, two sisters, a half brother and you, her real brother."

"Sounds like she's got more family than she needs."

Carrie looked him straight in the eye, her expression serious. "I don't think one ever has enough family." Then she lowered her head and began reading a piece of paper she'd snatched from the printer.

There was something in her face, some tone in her voice that made him think she might not have family, that she might be all alone. Like he'd been for so long. "Do you have family?" he asked.

Her head snapped up but she didn't look at him. "That doesn't matter." Then switching gears, she asked, "Did Vanessa tell you that your other sisters are married?"

"Yes, Rebecca and Rachel mentioned that in their letters." He couldn't help wondering about Carrie's marital status. She was a beauty, with big blue eyes to go along with her golden hair, which she wore in a casual style that suited her soft features.

"Rebecca is expecting her second—a baby girl—any day now."

Carrie's statement broke into his thoughts. "I didn't know that," he said, forcing his attention back on what she was saying.

"Joey, her son, is five and adorable."

"So he'll have a sister like Vanessa."

"Not exactly," Carrie said.

"Not exactly? Either Rebecca's husband is Joey's father, as well, or he's not." Jim stared at her, waiting for a response.

"He is. But when she was pregnant with Joey, she and Jeff lost contact and Rebecca never looked for him. When they accidentally found each other, he was already engaged to another woman. But he found a way to marry Rebecca."

"Good for him. But I think I'm going to need a chart to keep up with all of them."

Carrie laughed. It was a beautiful sound, he realized instantly. "There's only Rachel left. She's married to J.D. He's a rancher and he's terrific. A great guy."

"Are you attracted to him?" Jim asked, frowning. He didn't want anyone giving his sisters problems. And he could see how any man might be interested in the blonde.

The young woman stared at him, her mouth open. The expression should have made her unattractive, but it didn't. He guessed he had a weak spot for blue-eyed blondes.

"No! Absolutely not!"

"Then why did you say he was terrific?"

"Because he is. Especially the way he treats Rachel."

"Okay," Jim said slowly, watching her carefully. "Do they live in Dallas?"

"No, his ranch is in west Texas, five or six hours west of Dallas."

"Have you been there?" That would tell him how involved she was with his sister's husband.

"No," she said, frowning.

Before she could say anything else, Will came out of his office, putting on his jacket as he walked.

"We're going home, Carrie," he said. "Betty's putting on a big spread and she's expecting you to be there."

"I shouldn't intrude, Will. It's a night for family," Carrie said.

"You're family, honey, and don't you forget it," the man said as he stooped down to kiss her cheek. "Now, are you coming with us or do you have things you need to do? Dinner is at six."

"I'd better finish up a few things, but I'll be along for dinner." Carrie turned her eyes on him. "And...welcome home, Jim."

"Thank you." He could hear the sincerity in her voice. Still, there was something disturbing about the young woman. Perhaps because he'd actually found himself responding to her...?

CARRIE FORCED HERSELF to wait another hour at the office before she put away her work and went to her car. By now, she figured, Vanessa had had a chance to meet her brother. Maybe even Rebecca had gotten there, too, though Rachel probably wouldn't arrive until tomorrow.

She couldn't imagine the joy the three sisters would feel upon seeing their long-lost brother. She could hardly believe she'd met Jim herself, though she'd certainly dreamed about their first encounter countless times.

In the past year she'd had a lot of fantasies about Jim, all of them with her as a costar. She'd even started having conversations with his picture in which she'd imagined his responses, his smiles...his touch. In her fantasies, that tight-jawed look in his face relaxed, revealing a wealth of emotions.

Had she been wrong? The real Jim seemed as stoic and unemotional as his photo. But maybe that was to be expected under the circumstances. Once he was in the circle of family, surely he'd emote. No one could hold back for long in the Greenfield house. She knew how loving they were. After all, over the past year and a half they'd become her family, too, especially since both her parents were now gone.

When she reached the Greenfield house in the Highland Park suburb of Dallas, she went to the front door, an unusual occurrence. Since she and Vanessa had found each other again, she visited frequently, but usually through the back door.

When the door opened, Betty stared at her. "What are you doing ringing the doorbell, Carrie? Get yourself in here."

Carrie kissed the housekeeper's cheek. "I didn't want to intrude. Has everyone gathered to meet Jim?"

"No. We can't find Vanessa or Rebecca. We called the law office and her husband's gone, too."

"Maybe the girls went shopping for the baby. Did you try their cell phones?"

"No answer."

"Oh, my. Is the captain still here?"

"A'course. Will had to practically tackle him to keep him from leaving. Miz Vivian hasn't woken up, either. She's sleeping a long time."

"I'm up, Betty," called Vivian as she reached the first floor.

"Miz Vivian, guess who's here?"

"I can see. Hi, Carrie. How are you?"

"Vivian, I'm not who Betty means. Jim is here."

"Jim? Here? Where is he?"

Carrie looked at Betty even as she took Vivian's arm. She could feel the excitement running through Vivian.

"In the library," Betty said and preceded them down the hall and opened the door.

Carrie followed Vivian in, eager to see her reaction to Jim.

The man immediately stood, and Vivian didn't hesitate. She did what Carrie had wanted to do. She rushed forward and wrapped her arms around him.

Will chuckled. "Jim, this exuberant woman is my wife and Vanessa's mother."

Carrie could see the awkwardness Jim was experiencing. He hadn't expected a woman he'd never met to embrace him and press her head against his chest.

Finally, Vivian took a step back and smiled up at him as she cupped his cheek with one hand. "Oh, I'm so excited. We didn't think you'd be here for a few more months. This is so wonderful! Did Vanessa cry? She does that when things get too emotional."

Will responded to his wife's question. "Honey, we haven't been able to find Vanessa or Rebecca."

"Can't find them? That's ridiculous, Will! You're a private eye."

"I've called everyone I can think of. Jeff's office doesn't know where he is, either."

"Where's Joey? He should be getting out of kindergarten now. What if—"

"We sent Peter over to their house to wait for him to come home," Will assured her, mentioning Betty's husband, who also worked for them.

"We need to call the hospitals. Something may have gone wrong with Rebecca!"

Before they could call, the telephone rang. Will answered, then listened. "Okay, thanks, Bill. We'll be there in a few minutes."

He hung up the phone. "You were right. That was Bill, Jeff's partner. Rebecca went into labor while she and Vanessa were shopping. She's at Presbyterian."

"Good heavens!" Vivian exclaimed. "Everything's happening at once. I'll get my purse. Carrie, can you call Rachel?"

Carrie nodded, but she couldn't take her eyes off Jim. He looked like an inmate waiting for the right moment to break out.

Sure enough he said, "I'll check in with you tomorrow, Will," and edged toward the door.

Vivian ordered, "Stop!"

Jim came to an abrupt halt. "Yes, ma'am?"

"Do you have a fear of hospitals?" Vivian asked gently.

Carrie almost laughed aloud at Jim's confused expression. "No, ma'am."

"Then come with us. Rebecca will be thrilled that you've arrived in time for the birth of her second child." She tucked her hand into Jim's arm and dragged him out of the library.

Will grinned at Carrie and offered his arm. "I'm afraid you're stuck with me, Carrie, since Vivian captured the captain. Shall we go?"

"Yes, but we'd better tell Betty about Rebecca and to put dinner on hold."

"Good thinking. It may be a long night."

VIVIAN HAD INSISTED they all ride in the same car. On the way, Carrie had called Rachel, but Rebecca had already called her. Rachel and her husband were flying in.

Vivian hadn't stopped talking since she met the captain. "What a wonderful surprise to find you here, Jim. The girls will be so happy!"

Jim was sitting in the back seat beside Carrie. She had yet to see him relax, or to see him smile. She wanted him to be happy to be with his family again, but she wasn't sure what his response was yet. They were fairly overwhelming. Maybe it was too much to expect him to show his emotion so soon.

When they reached the hospital, Jim tried to hang back, but Vivian insisted he escort her. "The second floor is for maternity," she announced as they entered the elevator. "I know because our baby was born here five months ago. J.D. proposed to Rachel in the waiting room that night, too."

Carrie caught Jim's glance at her, as if he was acknowledging what she'd earlier told him. Either that or asking her to rescue him, she thought with a grin.

When they reached the waiting room, there was no one there. Vivian hurried up to the nurse's desk. The nurse told her what room Rebecca was in.

"But she already has two people in there. You should wait until one of them comes out."

Vivian turned to her family. "I'll go get them. It won't take but a minute. Wait right here, Jim."

Jim backed away as soon as Vivian disappeared. "I'm not sure I'll be welcome tonight. Perhaps I should go to the hotel and—"

"You seem uncommonly fond of your hotel room," Will teased.

Jim shrugged his shoulders. "Compared to my normal accommodations, it's pretty special."

Carrie felt she had to speak. "Jim—I mean Captain Barlow," she hurriedly said when he raised his eyebrow, "Vivian would be terribly hurt if you left. And Vanessa would cry. Please stay."

His deep brown eyes looked into hers, as if questioning her honesty. Finally he gave her a nod. "I'll wait."

He was a man of few words, Carrie decided, but she nodded in return, adding a smile. At least he'd agreed to stay.

Will guided him toward some of the seats. "You must get tired of standing at attention so much," he said.

"Not really," Jim said stiffly, still standing.

Carrie desperately wanted to know more about this man. Though it was none of her business, she asked, "What made you leave the marines now?"

She thought he was going to dive for a foxhole to avoid answering her question. But she kept her gaze focused on him, hoping he would explain himself.

Finally he said in a low voice, "I'd been thinking about getting out for a while now. I was afraid I'd die before I saw my sisters again. I'd already been wounded twice. I figured the third time would kill me."

A chill shot through Carrie. She'd often found herself worrying about Jim's safety. She'd listened more closely to the news about the Iraq war, fearing that one day she'd hear that Jim had been killed. It seemed they'd shared the same thoughts.

Just as Jim started to sit down, they all heard rapid footsteps coming down the hall. Jim's gaze fixed on the door where Vivian had disappeared.

Carrie was amazed. She thought she saw fear in his eyes. A man who had faced down the enemy, had been decorated with many medals, was frightened to face his baby sister?

Vanessa appeared in the doorway and came to an abrupt halt. She stared at Jim for a long minute. Then with a sob, she charged forward just as Vivian had done, her arms extended. Once again, Jim found himself holding a woman in his arms.

Jeff followed Vanessa, but he only extended one arm.

Awkwardly, Jim extracted his right hand from Vanessa's embrace and shook Jeff's hand.

"I'm Jeff Jacobs, Rebecca's husband. I'm glad to meet you. And Rebecca is waiting for you to come in and visit with her, if you don't mind."

Vanessa didn't turn loose of Jim, but she reared back so she could look up at him, tears streaming down her face. "Just promise you'll come right back," she said. "I wouldn't let you go, but Becca is suffering."

Jim stared at his sister and shook his head. "I didn't expect— You're beautiful, Vanessa. You were so little the last time I saw you."

"Wait until you see Rebecca and Rachel together," Vanessa bragged. "They're the real beauties."

Carrie protested. "You could be a triplet, Vanessa, and you know it."

"You remind me of Mom," Jim told his sister, awe in his voice.

Vanessa started blinking furiously to hold back more tears. She buried her face in his chest again, then she stepped back. "Go see Becca, and I'll try to get myself under control before you come back."

JIM HOPED Vanessa stopped crying. If she didn't, he might end up crying, too, and that would be embarrassing.

Jeff looked at Jim out of the corner of his eye. "Rebecca is a little emotional right now, so don't be surprised if she cries, too. All three girls have been anxious for you to come home."

"Why?" Jim blurted his innermost thoughts. "They don't know anything about me. I failed them. The only sibling I managed to keep in touch with was Wally, and I got him killed."

"Man, they idolize you and are so happy you've come. They don't expect you to jump through hoops or be a superhero. They just want their brother."

Jim drew a deep breath. Then he muttered, "Thanks." He wasn't sure if he believed the man, but he gave Jim a little more courage to face Rebecca.

Jeff opened the door. "Here he is, honey."

Rebecca, a dark beauty like Vanessa, sat up in bed and extended her arms, too. Jim wasn't a slow learner, so he hugged her in return. Nor was he surprised when tears ran down her cheeks. Her reaction was brought to an abrupt halt by a labor pain. Jeff hurried to the other side of the bed and took her hand, telling her to take short breaths.

Once it had passed, Jim leaned over and kissed her forehead. "Concentrate on your baby right now. I'll be around when you've delivered."

"Okay, but promise you won't disappear," Rebecca barely managed to get out before another contraction hit.

Jeff looked at Jim. "Would you ask the nurse to step in here?" he asked calmly.

Jim, however, could see the panic in his eyes, so he hurried out and found the nurse. Then he returned to the waiting room.

Chapter Two

"You didn't stay long," Vivian said, back in the waiting room.

"I think her pains have increased."

Vivian's attention transferred from him to Rebecca's situation. She hurried back to Jeff and Rebecca.

Jim frowned. "She's not Rebecca's mother, too, is she?"

Vanessa shook her head. "No, but she felt like she should've been. She wanted to adopt all of us, but her late husband wouldn't let her. So when we find any of you, she kind of adopts them with her heart. Besides, Becca doesn't have a mother around."

"Did her adoptive mother die?"

"No," Vanessa said, her lips pressed together.

Jim didn't ask any other questions. It was obviously not a happy situation. And he appreciated the support Vivian was giving his sister.

"How long will she be in labor?" he asked.

Will shrugged his shoulders. "I'm not sure, but Vivian said it's supposed to be shorter with your second child."

"Oh, I'd forgotten Rebecca had another child. Joey, right?"

"That's right. And you wouldn't have forgotten him if you'd met him. He's adorable," Vanessa said.

"Carrie mentioned him earlier." He looked at Carrie, nodding in gratitude. Their earlier conversation had helped him deal with the family. It helped to know someone who wasn't family, too. After all, he'd gone from having no family to having more than he could comprehend. Carrie seemed to understand how overwhelming it could be. He could look at her and center himself. He'd never felt that before with anyone.

"Come sit down, Jim," Will suggested again. "We may have a long wait."

"So everyone's staying until the baby is born?" Jim asked, a little surprise in his voice.

"We wouldn't miss it for anything," Will assured him and patted the chair next to him.

As soon as Jim sat down, Vanessa grabbed the chair on the other side of him.

"When did you arrive?" Vanessa asked.

"Around three, I think." He looked at Carrie for confirmation. "I arrived earlier at the airport, but I rented a car and found a hotel room."

"A hotel room? You're staying with us, aren't you?" Vanessa demanded.

"I don't want to be a problem," Jim said.

Will just shook his head. "I knew she'd react that way."

"Look, I just wanted to see you, Vanessa. You and Rebecca and Rachel. I don't intend to impose on you." He hadn't really made plans for his future, but he had a fat savings account and time to look around for what he wanted to do.

"Will, make him stay!" Vanessa exclaimed.

"Honey, I can't do that if he doesn't want to. Maybe your mother can talk him into it."

Jim didn't have anything to say about that, but Vanessa did. She blew out a sigh of relief. "Of course. Mom will take care of it."

It was Will's turn to ask him a question. "What do you plan to do now that you're out of the marines?" he asked.

Carrie took a seat and held her breath, waiting for the information she'd wanted to hear. Like his sisters, she didn't want to lose touch with Jim, even though she didn't have that right. But he'd been in her mind, in her dreams and fantasies, for so long. How could she let go of him now?

"I don't know. I'll have to get out the want ads and see if there's anything I can do."

"You handy with a gun?"

Jim frowned. He didn't know exactly how to answer that. "I'm a fair shot. I'm no gunslinger, though."

"Good. How are your computer skills?"

"Good. I majored in computer science."

Will's eyebrows shot up. "Excellent! I suppose you can handle yourself in a fight?"

"Just what do you have in mind, Will?"

"Have you thought about working as a private investigator?"

"You mean, like you?" Jim asked, surprised.

"Yeah, like Carrie and me."

Jim looked at the young woman. So she wasn't a receptionist, as he'd first thought. But she didn't appear particularly muscular. In fact, she looked quite feminine… and pretty, not that that mattered in her line of work.

He responded to Will, "No, I haven't."

"Well, I need another man in the firm. I don't like to travel out of town with Vivian and the baby at home, and I'm not comfortable sending Carrie every time. I could offer you a job, see if you like the work."

"You don't have to find me a job, Will. I'll find something. I figured security work."

"I can't see you as a security guard at a mall or a bank. Think about it. We'll talk again in a couple of days."

There were more rapid footfalls, only from a different direction. Then a young woman dashed into the room, followed by a cowboy. Jim didn't need anyone to tell him Rachel had arrived. He shot to his feet.

Rachel threw on the brakes and stared at him. Then she looked at Vanessa. "Is that Jim?"

"Yes, it is. He arrived today."

This time Jim was prepared. He opened his arms as Rachel flew into them. He was beginning to think he was getting quite good at welcoming his sisters. Too bad he didn't have any more of them.

He looked at Carrie out of the corner of his eye, over Rachel's dark head. She was the only woman he'd met since his arrival who *hadn't* hugged him. That was too bad.

"We thought it would be months yet!" Rachel exclaimed as she took a step back, tears streaming down her face. She whirled around to a brown-haired man who came in behind her. "J.D., it's my brother, Jim."

"I figured," the young man drawled as he stuck out a hand to shake Jim's. "J.D. Stanley."

"This is my husband, J.D. We just flew in from west Texas. I was going to drive in tomorrow, but J.D. insisted we fly. I'm so excited you're here!"

Then she must have remembered why she'd come and she asked, "Have you heard anything about Rebecca?"

"Mom just went back," Vanessa replied. "Her pains started coming faster."

Just then, Vivian came running back in. "Rebecca and Jeff just went into the delivery room. I'd better call Betty after all. Looks like we'll be home for dinner. And Joey will want to know what's happening."

"You didn't say hello to Rachel and J.D.," Will said, taking his wife by surprise.

"I can't believe you arrived so quickly." She hugged both of them. "We'll need to tell Betty to add two more for dinner."

Will looked at his watch. "Better tell her around seven for dinner. I wouldn't count my chickens before they're hatched," he said with a chuckle. "And ask how Danny's doing," he added. Then he looked at Jim. "That's our son."

Jim nodded. He hadn't forgotten. He sent a grateful look toward Carrie. According to her earlier explanations, he figured, he'd now met all the family.

When Vivian finished her phone conversation, she turned back to her husband. "Danny's fine. And Joey's so excited, he couldn't talk long. Betty was taking cookies out of the oven."

J.D. laughed. "That boy's got his priorities right."

Rachel slapped his arm. "Shame on you."

"Don't worry, honey," J.D. said, giving her a brief kiss. "I'd choose you over cookies anytime."

Vanessa looked at Jim with a grin. "They're newly-weds. Just ignore them."

"Rebecca's labor seems to be so fast this time. The doctor said that was normal for a second baby." Vivian looked at her husband, and apparently Will seemed to know what she was thinking at once.

"Don't even think about it, Viv. We were lucky the first time. I don't intend to push our luck." He kissed her and Jim could see the concern in his eyes.

"They're kinda newlyweds, too," Vanessa told Jim with a sigh.

"You feel a little left out?" he asked her quietly.

"Yeah. But I have a good friend in Carrie. We met our freshman year at SMU."

Carrie smiled at Vanessa, nodding. It seemed a little strange to Jim that Carrie, who appeared to work for a living, was friends with a young lady who apparently had her way paid for her. But that was none of his business.

Of course, they were both beauties. They had that in common.

Vivian jumped up from her seat to pace the room. "I'll be so glad when the baby's here. What did they decide to name her?"

Vanessa shrugged her shoulders. "They have several names picked out, but I don't think they wanted to make a final decision until they met her."

Rachel was smiling. "Rebecca sent me a picture of the sonogram."

Will grinned. "Yeah. She showed it to all of us, including Joey. He wasn't impressed!"

"He said she didn't look like Danny," Vivian said with a smile.

"Maybe she'll look like her mama did when she was a baby," Jim said softly, struck by how strong and vivid the memory was. In his mind's eye he could see Rebecca as a baby, her full head of dark hair, her pink face scrunched up as she cried. He could never tell her apart from her twin, Rachel. But his parents could.

"Yes, she and Rachel were pretty babies, just like Vanessa," Vivian said. She put a gentle hand on Jim's forearm. "We have a picture of all of you just before the accident."

Jim frowned. The accident that took their parents and shattered their happy home. How many times had he thought about that day? How many times had he thought of what it'd be like now if his parents were still alive, or if he'd managed to keep all the kids together?

"I'd love to see the picture," he told Vivian.

Rachel spoke up. "You don't have a picture of all of us?"

"No. They only packed a few of our clothes." Jim paused and looked down at his clenched hands. He'd never forget that day the social services worker came and took them from the house. He'd tried so hard to be brave, but the tears had fallen freely when he'd left the house that last time.

"I remember David had a teddy bear that he slept

with all the time. They left it behind. I heard he cried a lot…." He couldn't prevent the pang of guilt that jabbed him at the memory. "Then I didn't hear anything else about him after that. Finally my foster mother told me someone had adopted him."

Vivian reached out to cover his clenched hands and gave him a sympathetic smile when he looked at her.

Will sat up. "Did she give you any details? Whether it was a local adoption…"

He shook his head. "She said to stop worrying about David, that a lady had come to get him and she and her husband adopted him. That's all."

"Sounds like it might have been local," Will said slowly.

"Or it could've been a lie just to stop me from bugging her about him," Jim said quietly, his jaw tight. That would have been like his foster mother.

Vivian stared at him. "But, Jim, you were only nine. Of course you couldn't do anything."

Jim shot her a sharp look and couldn't keep the anger from his voice. Anger at himself. "I was the oldest. I was supposed to take care of my brothers and sisters."

"I'm sure you were a big comfort to Wally," Rachel said softly.

Jim shrugged. "Yeah, right. I didn't get to see him but once a month. Then when I got older, we talked on the phone every once in a while." His expression darkened with the memory. "Then he followed me into the marines…and died. Some comfort."

"But that wasn't your fault," Vanessa cried.

He turned to look at his youngest sister. "He joined so we could be together. It was my fault. We—"

Jim's explanation was interrupted by Jeff Jacobs. He ran into the waiting room, dressed in scrubs with tiny footprints on them.

"She's here!" he announced. "She's perfect and Becca is, too. They're moving them to our room now, and you can all come see our baby."

Everyone stood and followed Jeff out the door.

"We don't have anything to give them," Rachel exclaimed. "Honey, could you run down and buy some flowers from the gift shop?"

J.D. agreed to go purchase flowers.

"I'd better go with you," Jim said. "I don't have anything for them, either."

Before anyone could protest, Jim and J.D. hurried away.

Carrie was about to back off when she saw Vivian clutch her husband's hand. "I thought I was going to burst into tears when he talked about protecting his little brothers. He was only nine!"

"I know, dear." Will gave her a hug. "We'll give him more family than he ever dreamed of."

"If that's what he wants," Carrie said with a frown. She had sensed discomfort in Jim, as if she'd known instinctively that he wouldn't want anyone's sympathy. She hoped those feelings would go away, but she wasn't sure. After all, he'd been alone for a long time now.

Vanessa asked, "What do you mean, Carrie?"

"I think he may be a little overwhelmed with so much

going on." She thought he was more than overwhelmed. He'd wanted to meet his sisters—three people—and now here he is in the midst of a big family.

"We'll work it out, Carrie," Will assured her. "But you're right. It is different for him."

"But he's happy about finding us, isn't he?" Vanessa asked.

"Yes, dear, he is," Vivian hurriedly reassured her. Then she muttered to her husband, "And if he isn't, he will be soon!"

Will chuckled under his breath and urged them all into Rebecca's room. There, Rebecca and her baby were the center of attention.

"Oh, she's beautiful!" Vanessa exclaimed.

"Of course she is," Vivian said. "With Jeff and Rebecca as parents, she didn't have a choice." Vivian stretched out her arms. "May I hold her?"

Rebecca immediately agreed and passed the tightly wrapped bundle to Vivian. Vanessa and Rachel huddled around her, waiting for their turns.

Will shook Jeff's hand. "You made it through okay?"

"It was touch and go there in the delivery room, but the payoff was great. Isn't it a miracle?"

Will chuckled again. "You know it was for me. I never expected to have children. But then I never expected to love someone like Vivian, either. That was the first miracle."

Jeff nodded. "I know. I thought I'd lost Rebecca for good. Then one day I walked into my office and there she was. Then I found out about Joey. And now we have the new baby. Life just keeps getting better."

J.D. and Jim stepped into the small room, each handing the new mom a vase of flowers.

"Oh, how nice!" Rebecca exclaimed. "Jim," she prompted, "did you see the baby?"

"No, I haven't—" Jim stopped as Vivian handed him the infant. "No, I can't— I don't know how to take care of a baby."

"You don't have to do anything today. Just hold her," Vivian insisted.

Jim stood there, staring at the baby in his arms as she stretched and yawned. "She's...beautiful."

"Yes, she is," Rebecca agreed with satisfaction. "And do you want to know her name?"

Everyone drew closer, as if they thought Rebecca was going to whisper.

"We decided to name her after Jim," Rebecca said with a brilliant smile.

"You named her Jim?" Jim asked in astounded tones.

"No, silly. We named her Jamie. Jamie Ann Jacobs. What do you think?"

Everyone gave their approval except for Jim. He stared down at the tiny human in his arms, apparently unable to speak.

Carrie watched him hold the baby, his gaze fastened on the newborn's every feature. Suddenly, as if he felt her gaze, he looked at her.

"Did you get to hold her?" he asked softly.

"I didn't want to push," Carrie replied with a grin. "I'll see her later."

"Come look," he invited as Rebecca apologized for leaving Carrie out.

Carrie moved to his side. He looked even more handsome at that moment—a large, powerful man holding a tiny baby. "She's so small," she whispered.

Jim nodded. "Yeah, but she's got a lot of potential."

"And a lot of family," Carrie added with a smile.

After the baby was returned to her mother, Vivian told them it was time they went home and gave Jeff time with Rebecca before he followed them. "After all, he needs to see Joey tonight."

Jeff sat down on the bed and put his arm around his wife. "That's right. Tell him I'll be there after Rebecca goes to sleep. And I'll bring him in the morning to see his baby sister."

With calls of goodbye, the others left the room. Rachel asked if someone could give her and J.D. a ride because they didn't have a car. Vanessa volunteered at once.

"We'll see you at the house," Vivian said.

Carrie noticed that Jim seemed to hang back on the short walk to the car. She kept looking over her shoulder to be sure he was following.

They got in the car and started the drive back to the house. Vivian sighed. "My, it's always a relief when a baby arrives healthy."

Jim remained silent in his side of the backseat.

"Are you two hungry?" Vivian asked, looking back.

Jim nodded. After a minute he said, "Yes, I am. I missed lunch."

Vivian gasped. "Why didn't you say something?"

"There wasn't time. Besides, I've gone without meals before. It's no big deal."

"We'll have dinner as soon as we get home," Vivian

assured him. Then she took out her cell phone and dialed the housekeeper. After giving rapid-fire instructions, she clicked off the call and smiled over her shoulder at Jim. "Betty was appalled. She doesn't like for anyone to miss a meal. She'll probably meet you at the door with hors d'oeuvres."

"I don't want to be any trouble," Jim replied.

Carrie thought if he moved any closer to the car door, he'd open it and escape. He looked so uncomfortable.

To make him feel better, she said, "It's true. Betty lives to feed a hungry man. If Will hadn't married Vivian, she would've started carrying food to his apartment."

Jim's laugh was strained.

"She's right, Jim," Will said. "And nothing pleases Betty more than compliments. That's a good thing to remember." As he finished speaking, he slowed down to pull into the driveway of their home.

Vivian took Jim's arm again and led the way into the house. Betty met them, telling Jim she had hors d'oeuvres ready in the morning room. "You come right in, you poor man."

"Thank you, Betty," Jim said.

"They should be right behind us, Betty," Will told her.

"No matter. This man needs nourishment at once."

Jim selected a sausage roll off the plate Betty offered. He took a bite and said, "These are great, Betty."

He was a quick learner, Carrie chuckled to herself as she saw Betty beam at his compliment.

When the rest of the family arrived, the housekeeper herded them all into the dining room. Carrie was seated next to Jim, who was barraged by questions from his curious sisters and Vivian. Even though Carrie had only met the man hours ago, she seemed to be able to read his mind. Surrounded by so much family, he was overwhelmed, even downright scared. She sympathized with Jim, though there was little she could do.

After the meal, when everyone returned to the morning room for coffee, Jim remained standing by the doorway. She knew what he was up to.

As if on cue, he said, "I really enjoyed meeting all of you. Be sure and thank Rebecca for me. I hope to see you again sometime, after I've gotten settled in." And with that, he turned on his polished heel and left.

As everyone sat there, stunned, Carrie looked at Will, who nodded his head. At his unspoken direction, she knew what she had to do.

JIM CLOSED his hotel room door soundly and leaned against it. He let out the breath he'd been holding since he walked into Will Greenfield's office earlier that day.

He was exhausted. He'd had long days and nights of combat that hadn't left him this tired. Then again, the enemy didn't frighten him the way his newfound family had, he thought wryly.

He was glad he'd found his sisters. They were everything he'd imagined them to be all this time. Beautiful, kind, generous. Exactly the way his parents would've wanted them to grow up.

But he was just as glad that he'd been able to leave them in Highland Park and return, alone, to his hotel. He was so different from them. He couldn't live the lifestyle they lived. He couldn't open himself up the way they had with each other. It was better for him to put some distance between himself and them right away.

As if that was settled, he moved away from the door and went into the bathroom to get ready for bed. A knock on the door interrupted his progress. Innately cautious, he peered through the peephole.

He couldn't believe his eyes.

Throwing the door open, he demanded, "What are you doing here?"

Chapter Three

Carrie mustered her courage and looked him straight in the eye. The whole way over here she spent convincing herself she was doing the right thing by getting involved in Captain James Barlow's life. Their client had hired Greenfield and Associates—thus, her—to find him, so after all, he *was* her business. And that was the only reason she found herself at Jim's hotel room door. Business.

It had nothing whatsoever to do with how her heart sped up upon seeing him for the first time without his dress uniform jacket.

She cleared her throat and replied to his question. "I'm following orders."

"Whose orders?" Jim snapped.

"Will didn't want you to disappear. Your sisters have been waiting a long time for their big brother to come home." She made no move to enter his hotel room, but also made it clear she wasn't going away until she had her say.

"I said I'd see them after I've settled in. I need to find a job and a place to live."

"Will and Vivian would be glad to have you stay there with them. They have plenty of room," Carrie said, but she already knew the answer.

"I won't sponge off my sister's family. You don't live with them, do you?"

"No, of course not."

"Then you understand," he said, staring at her.

"Are you going to talk to Will about working with us?"

Jim sighed and stared down at her. "I don't know."

"He was serious when he said we needed help. We've got contracts with three different insurance companies and the cases are piling up."

"I need some time to adjust. And I'm used to making my own way." His voice was almost a growl.

"So did Rachel and Rebecca, but they became part of the family. And they all want you to do the same."

She watched his face, seeing various emotions in his eyes. Most of all, she wanted to hug him and reassure him. He didn't seem to grasp how much his family wanted to love him.

But she couldn't tell him. After all, she wasn't family. Nor could she hug him like his sisters had done. All she could do was try to maintain some contact with him. "Is it all right if Will calls you in the morning?"

"I guess so, but he doesn't need to give me a job."

"We need help, Jim. Truly," she said earnestly.

"I'll talk to him, but I'm promising nothing."

"I'll tell him." She'd pushed him as far as she could, she thought. He'd given his word to at least speak to Will, and Carrie's fantasy Jim would never break his word. So she said good-night and turned to walk away.

She could feel his eyes on her as she walked down the hall. Just before she entered the elevator, she looked back at him and gave him a warm smile.

His expression didn't change.

AFTER SHE REACHED her apartment, she called Will. "He's staying at the Holiday Inn in room #512. He agreed to speak with you in the morning, but he said you didn't need to give him a job."

"Thanks, Carrie. You did just what I wanted. I think it's going to be a while before he feels comfortable with the family. But we don't want to lose touch with him."

"I agree."

"Why don't we both take him to breakfast in the morning? I think you can help talk him into trying out the job."

"Me? I'll be glad to go with you, but I doubt it matters to Jim what I think."

"I'll meet you at the office at eight-thirty. Then we'll go pick up Jim."

"Okay, see you then."

Carrie hung up the phone and immediately moved to her closet to figure out what she was wearing tomorrow to impress Jim.

"You're being ridiculous!" she exclaimed, but she didn't stop until she found her favorite red suit and a new blouse she'd bought last week. She was glad that finally, in the last few months she had extra money to spend on her wardrobe.

It had taken her an extra couple of years to graduate college because she'd had to go part-time after her father's sudden death. Then her mother had been sick, which had drained her of both time and money. But it had been worth it because she'd had time with her mother that she wouldn't trade for any size bank account.

The luckiest thing that had ever happened to her had been to go to work for Will Greenfield.

Five years ago she'd come to work for him as a part-time receptionist, while she was in school. Then she began to handle some of the investigation work, the easier things that Will didn't have time for. Over time, her involvement deepened until she was working full-time as a P.I.

Throughout it all, Will treated her as a member of his family—which at the time had only consisted of himself. Then he'd met Vivian, who happened to be the mother of her former best friend. Carrie had simply walked away from Vanessa, leaving her in the dark about the events that had changed her life so completely.

With her father's death, her life had fallen apart like a house of cards. She no longer could afford tuition or new clothes or even the car her dad had bought her. She'd settled his bills by selling everything they had. Then she'd bought a cheap car and moved her and her mother into an apartment.

She still lived there.

But now she had her friendship with Vanessa back, and Will and Vivian in her life. And for the past year since she'd gotten involved in finding Vanessa's siblings, she had Jim. The fantasy Jim anyway. From the moment she'd seen his picture, his face had spoken to her. She felt like she knew him—intimately.

She was definitely attracted to him.

But that was the fantasy Jim, she reminded herself. The fantasy Jim opened himself up to her, allowed her to love him. But the real Jim…? So far he remained the stoic soldier returning from war.

Carrie laid out her clothes for the morning and finally went to bed, in the arms of a strong-jawed fantasy man.

JIM AWOKE LATER than he'd expected. He attributed it to the airline travel yesterday, and meeting his family for the first time.

When he emerged from the shower, the phone in his room was ringing.

"Hello?" he answered.

"Jim, it's Will Greenfield. Have you had breakfast yet?"

"No. I'm running late this morning."

"How about you join Carrie and me downstairs in the coffee shop? I want to buy you breakfast."

"You don't have to," he said.

"I know I don't, but I want to discuss the job I mentioned yesterday. I figure breakfast is the least I owe you if you'll listen to me."

Jim realized this man was determined. Until he heard his pitch, Will wouldn't leave him alone. He looked at his watch. "I'll be down in ten minutes."

"Fine. We'll have coffee waiting for you," Will promised.

It was the "we" that bothered Jim. He liked Will Greenfield. But Carrie… There was something there when he looked at her. Something that made him want to run in the other direction. He *should* run in the other direction he told himself. He didn't want to hurt her. And that was all he'd bring Carrie. Or any woman.

He dressed in black slacks and a royal-blue dress shirt. After all, he was no longer a soldier. When he looked in the mirror, it was strange to see himself in anything but khaki-green. Hoping he hadn't made a mistake in leaving the service, he picked up his billfold and his room key and headed for the coffee shop to face Will and Carrie.

When he entered the coffee shop, he looked around for Will Greenfield. But all he saw was Carrie Rand in a bright red suit, sitting in a booth. He frowned. He hadn't planned on a breakfast alone with Carrie. The less time he spent with her the better everything would be.

He considered returning to his room, but he'd agreed to breakfast. Reluctantly he walked over to the booth.

Carrie glanced up and gasped. "Jim! You're not wearing your uniform."

"No. I'm a civilian now," he said.

"But yesterday—" Carrie began.

"Was my last day in the military. I was traveling and it was easier to do so in uniform. Where's Will?"

"Um, he had an emergency call he had to take. Please sit down, Jim. He should be back shortly." Carrie signaled the waitress, who came to the table with a pot of coffee.

"Here's a hungry man," Carrie said with a smile. "Please pour him some coffee and maybe he'll be ready to order in a minute."

"I can order now, if you're ready," Jim said quietly.

"We've already ordered. I asked our waitress to hold

our order until you got here. Will said for us to go ahead and not wait for him."

"I'll take two eggs over easy, bacon, wheat toast and a short stack of pancakes."

"You certainly seem to know your mind, Jim. Will likes that."

"It's a habit the marines encourage," Jim said with a nod.

"I bet you were a fast learner, too," Carrie said, hoping to see Jim smile. She was sure a smile would increase his handsome quotient tremendously. Which was pretty incredible since she'd thought his stern appearance would be hard to beat.

Jim said, "Yeah."

He took a sip of his coffee. Then he noticed Carrie was drinking some kind of cola. "You don't drink coffee?" he asked.

"No. Diet Coke has caffeine, too. I drink it in the morning."

"I can see that in the summer, but in winter? Don't you want something hot?"

"If I feel cold, I drink hot tea," Carrie admitted. "I've got all the stuff for hot tea at the office. Sometimes I drink it there."

Jim looked at Carrie, puzzling over her relationship with Will. If Will hadn't shown how much he loved his wife and son, Jim might've thought they were having an affair. But Will seemed to act like a father to Carrie.

"So you like working for Will?"

"Yes, of course," Carrie said at once.

The waitress delivered their breakfasts and silence

reigned as they ate. Then, with a second cup of coffee in front of him, Jim looked at Carrie. "I'm still not sure if Will really has a job open or he's simply doing what Vivian wants him to do."

"Surely you don't believe—"

"Why else would he offer a job to a stranger?" Jim challenged her.

"You're not a stranger, Jim." Carrie nodded as Jim's gaze narrowed. "When Vivian first asked Will to find Vanessa's siblings, he warned her that they might not be the kind of people she would want Vanessa to know." She grinned. "Even he will admit he had low expectations of the rich. He figured Vivian thought Vanessa's siblings would be wealthy, like her."

"And they weren't?"

"We found Rebecca first, in Arkansas. She was a single mother with no help from her adoptive parents. They wouldn't even speak to her. She was providing for her son and continuing her college classes at night."

"So he invited her to Texas for a visit?" Jim asked.

"Not on your life. He wouldn't do that until he had figured out what was going on in her life. He went to Arkansas so he could interview her in person."

"That sounds safe."

"It was—until Vivian insisted on going with him. He told her she could go on the condition that she didn't reveal her identity. He told Rebecca she was his assistant."

"And she bought that?"

"She did until Vivian told her differently. Once Vivian met her, she insisted she come back to Dallas to meet her sister." Carrie smiled. "You see, Vivian sees with her heart, not her head. She's different from most rich people, and that's how she raised Vanessa, too."

"Is that when Will fell for her?" Jim asked, doubt in his voice.

"I don't think it was that fast. Will had been married before to a lady who wanted money, however she could get it. She divorced Will to marry a man almost twenty years older than her because he was wealthy."

"It makes it seem unlikely that he'd fall for Vivian, then."

Carrie chuckled. "He was a goner when he saw Vivian's generosity to Rebecca, offering her a home, helping her return to school full-time, becoming Joey's grandma. That's how she convinced Will without even trying. He realized she was different from the rich women he'd met in the past." Carrie paused, then gauging Jim's expression, said, "All of which is a long explanation so you'll understand that we know a great deal about you."

He looked confused. "I don't see how Will's love life explains why you already know a lot about me."

"It explains how Will wouldn't invite you to come meet your family unless he believed you wouldn't disappoint Vivian and your sisters. We've talked to many of your superior officers. We know about your returning to college to get a degree and moving up in the officer ranks. We've talked to men who served under you." Carrie stopped talking because of the frown on Jim's face.

"And what did you find that made you think I'd be a good P.I.?" he demanded.

"You're smart, decisive, caring, honest," Carrie said.

"You can handle yourself in a fight, you majored in computer science and you're a good friend."

"You already knew about my degree when Will asked about my computer skills?" Jim asked, one eyebrow raised.

Carrie had the grace to look a little embarrassed. "Yes. We weren't sure how you'd feel about having been investigated."

"I don't like it one damn bit!"

Carrie kept her gaze fixed on her plate, pretending to ignore Jim's glare.

"If someone you loved wanted to find a stranger, wouldn't you investigate the person before you introduced them?" Carrie asked gently.

After a moment of silence, Jim said, "Yeah, I would. But that doesn't mean I want to work as a P.I."

"Never said it did," Will agreed, suddenly appearing at the table. "But I hope Carrie explained everything to you. We need some help. If you don't agree to work for me, I'll have to find someone else." Will sat at the table and waved for the waitress to bring his breakfast.

"Tell me about the work."

Will began to tell him about cases they had pending, between bites, pointing out that most of their cases involved investigating people trying to trick the insurance companies. "Occasionally, we take cases that the police have given up on. Or cases like Vivian's."

"No divorce cases? No tailing cheating husbands?"

"I try to avoid them."

Jim looked at Carrie. "What do you do?"

"The same work as Will."

"You actually tail people?"

"Of course."

"You carry a gun?"

"Yes."

Jim raised his cup and took a long drink of coffee. Then he looked at Will. "How about a trial run? I'll work for you for a week, no pay. If I like the work, we'll talk."

"That's more than fair. Let's shake on it," Will said, extending his hand to Jim.

After shaking Will's hand, Jim extended his hand to Carrie.

Reluctantly, slowly, she gave him her hand, hoping he wouldn't realize she was shaking more than his hand. She had a thing about shaking hands. It told her a lot about a person. But she already knew about Jim. Shaking his hand only confirmed her attraction to him. To the real Jim.

"Well," Will said, "shall we go to the office? If you can catch on to what we do on the computer, Carrie has some fieldwork to do. You can use her desk."

Jim again looked at Carrie.

All she could manage was a nod agreeing with Will's statement.

"Are you going to stay here for the week? That will be kind of expensive." Will paused and then said, "Since you're working for free, you could stay with us. We really do have plenty of room."

"I don't think—"

"Then I'll have to pay you a salary for the first week."

"No, I—"

"Vivian will ask. She'd be horrified at my taking advantage of you."

"Fine. You can pay me minimum wage for the week. Until I catch on, that's all I'll be worth anyway."

Will blinked several times. Then he said, "It's a deal. But we'd still like to have you move in with us."

"That's very kind, but no thank you."

Carrie smiled. Jim had just proven her right. She'd told Will this morning she didn't think Jim would go along with his offer.

"So you're going to stay here?" Will asked.

"I'm going to look for an apartment, but I'll stay here until I find something." Jim stood. "I need to go get my jacket. I'll be right back."

Once Jim had left the table, Carrie grinned at Will. "I won that bet," she pointed out.

"Yeah, you did. I'd hoped I could persuade him."

"I know, for Vivian. But they'll get to see him often and he'll get used to a big family after a while."

"I guess it has been kind of sudden." He stood. "We'd better head for the office." He waved the waitress over for their bill.

"Can you show him what we need done on the computer?" Will asked as he paid.

"That shouldn't be a problem. It's not that difficult."

"Then what will you do?"

"Fieldwork, like you said."

"Nothing dangerous, right?"

Carrie shrugged her shoulders. "I have a couple of specific cases in mind."

"Which ones?" Will asked.

"The Moore case…and maybe the Riley case."

"No! I'll do that one, Carrie. I told you that one is dangerous. That man is amoral. He won't hesitate to kill anyone who's trying to stop him from getting his money."

"And that's why I have to do it. He would suspect you, but he won't suspect me."

"No. I won't allow you to go alone."

"Trouble in paradise?" Jim asked, coming up alongside them.

"Carrie wants to do something dangerous, and I won't let her," Will said firmly.

"It's obvious you just want to protect her," Jim said, raising one eyebrow.

"I am. But she thinks she has to protect me."

"Vivian made me promise," Carrie said with a light chuckle that defused the situation.

"Uh, I'm ready to go," Jim said, garnering Will's attention.

"Fine. Do you want to turn in your rental car? We could follow you and pick you up."

"No, thanks," Jim said, "I'll keep it until I buy a car."

"I'm just trying to save you some money," Will explained.

"I never said I was penniless," Jim protested.

Carrie stepped closer to the two men. "I think Jim can handle his personal life. Shall we go to the office?"

"Yeah," Will said. "Sorry, Jim. I'm used to— I try to take care of the family."

"I appreciate that, Will, but I'm pretty independent."

"Well, we'll see you at the office. You can follow us

if you want. Or better yet, Carrie can ride with you and show you how to find the office."

"I managed to find it yesterday, Will," Jim pointed out.

"Ride with him, Carrie," Will said, and walked off.

Chapter Four

"I'm sorry," Carrie said softly as they watched Will walk away.

"For what?"

"For Will forcing you to take me in your car. It was obvious you didn't want to."

Jim stared straight ahead, his jaw squared. "I never said that."

Carrie shrugged her shoulders. "You said it, just not in words. I know enough about people to read their body language."

"Is that so?"

He didn't sound impressed with her claim.

"Yes, but I won't bother to apologize again."

They got in his car and drove in silence.

Finally Jim spoke. "So, you like working for Will?"

"I work *with* Will," she said, leaving him in no doubt that she considered the partnership a reality.

"So you bought in?"

She stared at him. "Why did you ask that like you didn't believe my buying in was a possibility?"

"I didn't mean to. I asked that question because I was wondering how much money I'd need if I wanted to buy in, assuming the week goes well."

"Oh." Carrie turned to stare out the window.

"So you're not going to tell me?"

"I'm a junior partner, not a full partner. You'd have to discuss that with Will." She kept her face averted. She didn't want him to see the hope in her eyes. It might scare him away.

"Okay. I'll wait until the week is up before I talk to Will."

"Yes. That's a good idea."

"Okay. Why did Will try to get me to move in with him and Vivian?"

"Because Vivian really does think all Vanessa's siblings should have been part of their family. She wants the best for all of you."

"I'm an adult, not an orphan," Will protested. "That's not necessary."

Carrie shrugged again. "There's a spirit in Vivian that draws you to her. And she never sees the flaws. She acts like a mother to everyone. I appreciate her even more now since my mother is gone. I don't have any real family. But I have Will, Vivian and Vanessa and everyone that comes in contact with them."

"I don't need to be mothered," Jim said tightly.

"Don't hurt Vivian's feelings. That's the best advice I can give you."

"I don't look for ways to hurt people, Carrie. But I'm not used to being…involved in a family."

"I think you're not used to being loved," she replied.

His jaw clenched again. "It doesn't pay to love me! Ask Wally! Ask my parents! Ask my sisters! Ask Lani!"

"Who is Lani?" Carrie asked at once.

"Never mind." He wheeled the car into a parking space beside the office building where Greenfield and Associates was located. He threw the gearshift into Park and stepped out of the car as soon as Will pulled up next to them.

Clearly Jim was through talking.

"Is THAT IT?" Jim asked, frowning as he looked over Carrie's shoulder. After he'd met with Will, she'd taken a couple of hours to teach him how to use the computer to track down information.

"Yes," she explained, "but we redo many of our cases to determine activity. For example, if a man with back injuries that require him to be in a wheelchair buys a boat, we might want to revisit the subject."

"Are people that dumb?"

"They have to spend their ill-gotten gains somehow. And frequently, we'll find they collected on other insurance policies earlier. Repeat criminals."

"I gather they're not happy to be discovered."

"Right, but it's not our job to try the case. Just to provide evidence." She stood, forcing Jim to take a step back.

"This digital camera is as important a tool as the computer. We get photos that prove the subject isn't injured, and we send them over the Internet to the insurance company."

"All right. Now, how about I go with you this afternoon, to see how you operate?" Jim's voice was casual, as was his stance. But his eyes gave him away.

"No, thank you," Carrie said coolly. "I work best alone."

Jim took a couple of steps back, then he called to Will. "Will? Carrie doesn't want me to go with her. She thinks she'll be better alone."

Carrie knew what Will's response would be. She gathered her courage to resist his preference.

Sure enough, Will came out of his office. "Carrie, I think it would be a good idea for Jim to go with you."

"Especially since I'm checking up on Richard Riley?" Carrie said, staring at Will.

"Well, it wouldn't hurt to have someone with you," Will said reasonably.

"Will, if you don't think I can do my job, I'll have my resignation on your desk tomorrow." She drew a deep breath. "After I check on Richard Riley today!"

She picked up her files and headed for the door.

"Wait!" Will called.

Carrie didn't want to stop, But it was Will. "Yes?" she asked, turning around.

"Jim will promise to stay in the car. In fact, I insist he do so, since he's not licensed to carry a gun yet."

"You know we don't use guns to do our job," Carrie insisted.

"I know. But I like you to have one for emergencies." Will cleared his throat. "Just take Jim with you. Explain your approach and show him the files. He can read them while you're contacting our suspect. That's all, Carrie. You don't mind, do you?"

Carrie minded. Not because she thought Jim was going along to protect her. But because she wouldn't be at her best with the big man beside her. She was too conscious of him, too interested in his response.

But she didn't have a choice unless she really wanted to quit. And she didn't. "Okay, but he stays in the car."

The two men exchanged a glance that irritated Carrie, but they both agreed to her terms. So when she walked to her car, she had Jim alongside her.

"You're mad that I involved Will?" Jim asked after they'd gotten in the car.

"Yes," she said in a clipped tone.

"How else am I going to learn?"

Carrie flashed him an angry look. "This is not rocket science. The computer is the hard part and you thought it was simple. Sneaking up on people is a lot less complicated."

"Maybe. But I'm not used to that. In the marines, everyone knows you're a soldier."

Carrie just shook her head. "Richard Riley is the top file. You can start reading it."

Jim gave her a knowing look, but he did as she suggested.

Richard Riley claimed the injuries he'd sustained in a car accident had left him unable to walk, relegating him to a wheelchair. He'd sued the other driver for millions. But apparently the insurance company had reason to believe Mr. Riley was a fake, and they'd hired Greenfield and Associates to prove them right.

It didn't take long for Jim to figure out why Will thought the man might be dangerous. Not only had he bilked fifty grand from an insurance company five years ago, but he had numerous guns registered in his name. Besides, six-figure settlements made people antsy.

"No wonder the company wants you to investigate," Jim said, closing the file.

"Yes, they've been dragging their heels on paying, but Riley's attorney has arranged for settlement within a couple of weeks."

"So how are you going to approach him?"

"I'm not. I'm going to approach his wife. I have a cosmetic demo that I've used before. I knock on the door and ask if I can show her the latest trends in makeup."

"But you don't wear makeup."

She smiled. "I will when I go to their house."

They had reached the street that the Rileys lived on. Carrie parked three houses down, then reached in the backseat and brought out a pink case. When she opened it, she began applying makeup.

Jim watched her every move, making her nervous. In five minutes she was ready. "Remember," she told him, "you promised to stay in the car."

"Right. How long will you be?"

"Possibly half an hour, maybe longer."

JIM CHECKED HIS watch after Carrie had exited the car. It was two o'clock. He slumped down in the seat and picked up the next file.

Fifteen minutes later, there was still no sign of Carrie. He'd watched her enter the home, but he didn't know if the wife was home alone or with Riley. If Riley was suspicious, Carrie could be in danger.

What could he do? She'd said at least half an hour. He wouldn't be justified in going to the house and ringing the doorbell.

Stirring in his seat, Jim wanted to get out and at least stretch his legs. But he didn't dare. Too bad Carrie had one of those little economy cars. It was certainly nondescript, though, good for undercover work.

He studied the files some more, and when he felt as if he'd memorized them, he checked his watch, noting that Carrie had been gone twenty-eight minutes. He gave up any pretense of studying the files. Instead, he stared at the front door of the house Carrie had entered. As four minutes ticked off his watch, he grew more and more antsy.

Just when he'd seized the door handle, ready to ride to the rescue, Carrie came out of the house with a friendly wave to the woman at the door.

Then she walked up the sidewalk to the house next door and rang the doorbell.

Damn it! What was she doing?

There was obviously no answer there. Carrie did the same at the next house. Someone answered that door, and for several minutes Carrie talked to whomever answered the door. Then, with a wave, she headed toward the car.

Jim breathed a sigh of relief. Everything was all right.

When Carrie got in the driver's seat and stowed her makeup case in the backseat, Jim prodded, "Well?"

"I'm not sure."

"Did you see Riley?"

"No. The wife said his brother took him out. Apparently he does that every once in a while. The brother is supposed to be a big man who can lift Riley in and out of his wheelchair."

"Did you get his brother's name?"

"Of course I did," she said, looking down her nose at him. "It's Charles. I intend to be sure he can lift his brother. In the meantime, his wife said she couldn't buy anything until they got their insurance payment. Then they're going to take a vacation."

"Where?"

"I don't know yet. But I will. Mrs. Riley assured me her husband loves to buy their tickets online because he can get a better deal."

"But he won't have to worry about a deal if he gets that big check."

Carrie smiled. "People follow the same pattern, even if circumstances change."

"So you'll check on the size of his brother and watch for airline ticket purchases?"

"That's right. We garner our evidence piece by piece, until we have a complete picture."

"Sounds like it takes patience," Jim said with his gaze narrowed on something outside the car.

"That's right."

"And it doesn't bother you that you're constantly dealing with scum?"

"No. I think of myself as a policeman. Someone has to hold the line on decency."

"Okay. What do we do now? Are you going to visit the other two cases this afternoon?"

"No, I think I'll save them for another day. I want to

track down Riley's brother." She felt like she was on the verge of proving what she believed—that Riley was a fake. She'd been working on this case for a month now and anticipated the big fee the insurance company would pay to have this claim proven false.

When they got back to the office, Jim asked, "Mind if I watch?"

"Will might have something else you can do."

Jim frowned. "Trying to get rid of me?"

"Didn't you warn me to keep my distance?" she demanded, hoping her voice didn't sound as surly as she thought it did. She regretted her words almost at once.

His withdrawal was more than physical. His eyes went blank, his voice turned cold. "Right." Then he turned and knocked on Will's door. "Will, have you got a minute?"

Carrie stared as Jim entered Will's office and closed the door. She felt awful. She would like to become his friend, but her feelings weren't friendly. In her imagination, Jim would sweep her off her feet. Their eyes would have met over her desk and their attraction would have been mutual and instantaneous. In reality, instead of a come-hither look, his eyes told her to keep her distance.

The phone rang and Carrie answered. It was Vivian wanting Carrie to come to dinner tonight for Jim's first family meal.

"I'm not sure that's a good idea, Vivian. Our first day hasn't gone smoothly."

"Carrie, I want you to come. You haven't been over in a while."

"I was there last night, remember?"

"Yes, but there were so many of us. I lost track of you."

"Let me talk to Will first."

"Okay, but I'm expecting you."

Carrie said goodbye and hung up the phone. Then the door opened and Will, with Jim beside him, came out. "Carrie, can I talk to you while Jim tries out the computer?"

"Of course." She followed Will back into his office. He indicated she should sit down in front of his desk.

"How are things going?"

She dropped her gaze to her hands. "Fine."

"Jim seems to feel you don't want to work with him."

Carrie didn't look up, nor did she know what to say. Finally she answered honestly, as she always did. "It's—it's difficult having him around, but I'll adjust. If he stays and he gets his own cases and his own computer, it will be fine."

"Are you sure? We need the help, but I owe you a lot. You've hung with me a long time. If you can't work with Jim, then I'll help him find another job."

"No, Will. He's family. I'm not. I'll try harder to be…polite to him."

"I'd appreciate it, honey. I really do think he's going to be good at this job."

"Yes, I'm sure he will. If you don't mind, I think I'll go home early. That will give Jim time at the computer without me hanging over him."

"Sure. Do you feel all right?"

"Yes, of course. Oh, and Vivian just asked me to dinner, but would you tell her I can't make it? I've got other plans."

"All right. But it would be nice if you came to dinner tonight."

"Thank you, but I can't."

She slipped from his office before he asked more questions.

When he realized she had come out of Will's office, Jim started to get out of her chair.

"No, that's all right," she said. "I'm going home early. You can use the computer the rest of the day. I'll see you tomorrow."

"Carrie, are you going home because of me?"

"No. Yesterday was such a long day, and I've made plans for this evening, so I'm going to go home and have a bubble bath."

She got her purse out of the desk drawer and waved goodbye. If she'd had any more excuses, she'd have used them. But she was all out. Fighting tears that suddenly appeared in her eyes for no reason at all, she hurried to her car.

Better to get away from the handsome man she'd dreamed about for months now. It was so tempting to throw herself into his strong arms. But that was her dream, not reality. She had to fight those dreams.

When she reached her apartment, she sat down on the couch, unsure what to do with herself. Finally she pulled out the paper and looked at the movies playing. She chose a romantic comedy showing near her apartment. That was how she would spend her evening.

Anything to escape reality. The Jim Barlow of her dreams was a wonderful, accommodating man. The real

Jim Barlow was a stubborn, difficult man. He was intruding into her world, making her life unsettled. But while she was still fascinated with him, he wanted her to keep her distance.

She was being torn apart by her unreasonable emotions, longing to feel his arms around her, but reading his resistance in his eyes.

Maybe the film she chose would relieve her frustration.

PER HIS WIFE's instructions, via the phone, Will asked Jim to come to dinner. He immediately said no.

"You have other plans?" Will asked.

"No, but I ate dinner at your house last night."

"And it was so bad you can't bring yourself to come again?" Will asked, grinning.

"Of course it wasn't. Betty cooked it," Jim said, laughing in response. He knew what Will was doing. "You're not going to shame me into accepting. Besides, I need to look for a place to live. You yourself said it was too expensive to live in the hotel."

"Well, yeah, but Vivian and Vanessa might know of someplace nearby. Besides, Rachel and J.D. are leaving to go back home in the morning. They'd really like to see you again."

Jim stared at the man being so reasonable. Finally he said, "Okay, I'll come tonight, but I can't get in the habit of eating Betty's cooking every night. I'd double my weight if I did."

"I'll warn Vivian that it can't be a constant thing. Okay?"

Jim nodded. "Is Carrie coming?" He held his breath,

waiting for Will's assurance that Carrie would be present. No matter how he wanted to deny it, he was attracted to Carrie Rand. She impressed him with her strength, but at the same time, he was bowled over by her femininity. By her sexy curves and shapely legs. No matter how much he tried telling himself it was because he was in the military too long and had spent endless days and nights with men, he knew that was just an excuse. It wasn't any woman who attracted him. It was Carrie.

His disappointment was palpable when Will told him she wouldn't be there tonight.

"Does she usually turn down your invitations?"

"On occasion. She's allowed to have a life, Jim."

Jim thought about that idea as they walked down to their cars. "So Carrie has a...significant other?"

"Not that I know of," Will replied.

"So if you called her and said I wasn't coming, would she change her mind?"

Will stopped and faced Jim. "No, I don't think so. Carrie wants things to work out for you. There may be a slight adjustment period, but it will work out." He clapped Jim on the back. "Put Carrie out of your mind and come enjoy your family."

JIM WAS TRYING to do as Will had suggested, but as soon as he entered the Greenfield house, Vivian asked, "Where's Carrie?"

Will frowned. "She told me to tell you she said she had plans." He bent down to kiss his wife and launched right into the discussion Jim dreaded.

"By the way, Jim is looking for an apartment. Do you know of any in the area that have vacancies?"

Vivian stared at him with her big does eyes. "I was hoping you'd move here, Jim."

He slowly shook his head. "I appreciate the offer, Vivian, but I'm used to being independent. I'd appreciate any recommendations you might have."

"Well, we'd want it to be somewhere close. I'm not sure—"

Vanessa's entrance interrupted their discussion. "Jim! I wasn't sure Mom was telling the truth until now. I'm so glad you're here! It brightens my day—and it needs brightening. I took a test today that I'm sure I failed!"

Jim frowned, concern in his eyes.

To his surprise, Vivian laughed. "You'll have to get used to Vanessa's dramatics. She probably got an A on it. She always assures me she did horribly, then she brings home a good grade."

Jim looked at Vanessa. "Is that true?"

She gave a rueful grin and shrugged her shoulders. "Maybe."

"You can't do that to me. My heart can't take it," Jim said.

Vanessa looked stricken. "I didn't mean to upset you!"

"No, of course," Jim said, and, to even his surprise, he put an arm around Vanessa and hugged her. "I just want the best for my sisters, that's all."

"Wow," Vanessa said in surprise. "He's going to be an even tougher taskmaster than you, Mom."

"Good," Vivian said with a smile.

Vanessa looked at Jim. "Even when I was little, Mom always said if I did my best, it was okay. It always made me feel guilty if I hadn't."

"She's a smart lady." Jim smiled at Vivian.

"Well, now that we've got that settled, maybe Vanessa knows of some apartments," Vivian suggested.

"For whom?" Vanessa asked.

"For me, honey," Jim said. He raised a hand when Vanessa opened her mouth to protest. "I can't live here. I'm used to taking care of myself. So, do you know of any apartments in the area?"

A huge smile lit up Vanessa's face. "Actually, I do know of an apartment. And if you move into it, you'll have Carrie as your neighbor!"

Chapter Five

It wasn't Jim's fault.

Since last night Carrie had been telling herself those words over and over again. And she believed them. She knew whose fault it was that she'd eaten a hot dog at the theater and watched a silly movie, instead of dining on one of Betty's wonderful dinners and enjoying good conversation.

It was her fault.

She needed to stop reacting to Jim as if he were a long-lost lover instead of a stranger. When she'd gone to bed, she'd tossed and turned, trying to deal with her dreams and reality. She should've known better.

Promising herself that tomorrow would be different, she'd finally drifted off to sleep around one o'clock. Then she'd overslept and had to scramble to get to work by nine.

To her surprise, she was the first to arrive. She checked her desk to be sure everything was in its correct place. Then she chastised herself for being so possessive.

She made a fresh pot of coffee for Will and Jim, and

got a soft drink out of the small refrigerator. She hadn't had time for breakfast this morning.

The phone rang and she slipped into her chair to answer it. "Greenfield and Associates."

Will had decided on that name because it made his office sound bigger than it was.

"Oh, yes, Mr. Michaels. How may I help you?"

She twisted her chair around to turn on her computer as she listened to the man's complaints.

"Yes, I'm so sorry. We've had a particularly heavy load the past couple of weeks, but Will has added a new associate. I think he'll be terrific at helping lower the wait time."

After a pause, she said, "He's more than competent. He just got out of the marines and he's quite capable of handling any situation. His name? James Barlow.

"Yes, as soon as he's had a chance to study your files, I'll have him call on you so you can meet him. I think you'll be impressed." Another pause. "Yes, Mr. Michaels, I appreciate your calling. Goodbye."

"Nicely done, Carrie," Will said, standing in the doorway, Jim beside him.

Carrie recovered quickly. "Thank you. Jim, Mr. Michaels is with Liberty Insurance, one of our most important customers. He'd like to take you to lunch as soon as you've looked over his files." After a quick glance at Jim, she trained her eyes on some of the files on her desk. Pulling six of them out of the pile, she offered them to Jim. "I'm sure Will won't mind if you use one of the chairs in his office to look them over. And the coffee is ready."

Will added his consent, then said to Carrie, "I bought doughnuts. Bring your drink and come into my office."

Carrie would've preferred to take a pastry and return to her desk, but she'd joined Will too many times for him to accept that she was too busy.

Acting on her resolution from last night, she squared her shoulders and picked up her drink. Then she followed the two men to Will's office.

"We need to bring you up to date on some changes," Will said as he sat down.

Carrie's stomach heaved and she braced herself. He might have decided that she had to go. Jim was certainly a better risk than she because he was a big man.

"We decided to go ahead and order another desk and computer and whatever else is necessary for another investigator. We'll need it whether it's Jim or someone else, so it seemed silly to wait."

Carrie swallowed carefully. "I agree."

She could feel Jim's gaze on her, but she stared at Will, waiting to see what else he had to say.

"We ordered the desk this morning and paid a bonus to get it delivered this afternoon."

"Oh, good."

Will smiled at Jim. "See? I told you Carrie wouldn't be upset. Now, I think you and Jim should go get all the supplies he'll need, including some filing cabinets."

"I could do that by myself, and Jim could use my computer while I'm gone," she suggested, careful to keep the panic out of her voice.

"No. He may have some preferences that we don't know about," Will said with a grin. "I'm going to work on my computer while you're gone. Then I'll go out this afternoon when you're here to accept delivery on the desk and anything else you've bought."

"All right. Just let me make a couple of calls. Then I'll be ready to go." With a smile, she took her soft drink back to her desk, without ever having touched a doughnut.

Good thing. Having to play the role of disinterested person where Jim was concerned made her stomach a little queasy.

WILL LOOKED AT JIM, a smile of pride on his face. "See? I told you it was your imagination. She was selling you to Michaels when we came in. And she didn't object at all to our plans."

"And you think she was just having an off day yesterday?"

"Sure. We all have one every once in a while, especially ladies. But don't tell Vivian I said that."

"No, I won't. Nor Carrie."

"Right," Will agreed with a big grin. "You're catching on."

"We have women in the military now, too, Will."

"Oh, I guess so. Okay, here's the company credit card. Give it to Carrie."

"What limit do I have?"

"Get what you need. If you're worried about the price, ask Carrie. She handles everything for the office. That's why I want her to go with you. Bring back what you can carry and get the rest of it delivered today. Pay extra if you have to."

"Okay. By the way, Carrie didn't get a doughnut. Mind if I take one to her?"

"Of course you can. Take one for yourself, too."

"Nope. I had breakfast. I don't want to overdo it." Jim took a napkin and picked up a doughnut for Carrie. Then he went back to the outer office.

Carrie was on the phone, and he set the treat in front of her without a word. Then he leaned against the wall and scanned the files she'd given him, waiting for her to finish her calls.

She hung up the phone and picked up the doughnut. "Thanks, Jim. I'm a little hungry."

"Too bad you don't live with Will and Vivian. Betty would feed you."

"Yes, she would," Carrie said smoothly, not adding that she'd had many a breakfast at Vanessa's house.

Jim also handed her the credit card. "Will said to give this to you. He said you'd know what we could afford."

"Yes. Are you ready?"

Jim nodded, keeping an eye on Carrie's face. He still didn't believe she wanted him there. "Shall we use my rental?"

"No, I'd prefer to take my car."

He followed her out of the office to the parking lot.

"Did you have fun last evening?" he asked casually.

"Yes, thank you." Neither her tone nor her facial expression gave him any clue as to what she'd done with her evening.

"Vanessa was upset that you weren't there."

Carrie got behind the wheel of her little car before

she answered. "I guess that means I've been going over to their house too often."

"Why would you say that?" His knees were against the dashboard. As soon as he was sure he would have a job, he was going to buy a car. One big enough for him.

"I've been worrying about that lately. It's so easy to accept. Vivian and Vanessa are so welcoming, and Betty acts like you're two-timing her if you eat anywhere else."

"So what's the problem? They obviously enjoy your company."

"But I never invite them to my apartment for dinner. So I'm sponging off them." She turned on her blinker and pulled into the parking lot of a busy office-products store.

Jim got out, glad to stretch his legs. "I kind of thought you were avoiding me."

After one quick look his way, she started walking toward the store. "Of course not."

"I got the impression yesterday that you didn't want me here," he persisted, catching up with her so he could see her face.

She gave him a smile and a shrug. "I'm afraid I don't do change well. I'll adjust. You're going to be quite a help to us. In fact, if I don't mind my p's and q's, Will may shove me out the door."

"Is that what you're worried about?" he said, catching her by the arm. Feeling her tense up, he removed his hand. "You know better than that, don't you?"

"Yes. It was just a bad joke." She entered the store and grabbed a cart, immediately discussing supplies. For almost an hour, she kept the subject on business.

Jim had to admit he wouldn't have done the shopping as thoroughly or as efficiently without her. Soon she had a salesman walking the aisles with her. When they checked out, she didn't even bat an eye at the total.

The smaller items were in two big sacks and Jim picked up both of them. The rest would be delivered.

"I can carry one of those," Carrie protested.

"You've done all the work so far. This is the least I can do."

After they loaded the sacks into the backseat and got in the car, he said, "I can see why you're so valuable to Will. That shopping trip was impressive."

"Yes, it's a woman thing."

Jim eyed her sharply. "I wasn't implying that you couldn't do the rest of your job. I would imagine you'd be much better at certain deceits than me."

"Yes, women lie better than men, don't they?"

"Damn it! I was trying to pay you a compliment, not insult you."

She said nothing.

"I swear I didn't have this much difficulty getting along in the military with either men or women. What's the problem?"

She stopped at a red light. "I'm sorry, Jim. I'm not used to—to sharing. I'll try to be more agreeable."

She spoke in clipped tones, no emotion in her voice.

Jim couldn't figure out what the problem was. But he warned himself to be on his toes.

When they got back to the office, Jim spent half an hour organizing the supplies. He put them in a pile on the floor to await his desk.

Around noon, Vanessa arrived. "Carrie, how about lunch?"

"I'd love to, Vanessa, but someone has to stay here to await Jim's desk and supplies deliveries. Maybe another day," she added with a smile.

Instead of accepting her excuse, Vanessa stepped to Will's desk. "Can you and Jim stay here while Carrie and I go to lunch? Then she'll come back and wait for the deliveries while you two go?"

"Sure, that's fine with me." Will called out, "Is that okay with you, Jim?"

He agreed to the plan.

"Good!" Vanessa exclaimed. "Because I want to hear all about Carrie's new boyfriend!"

Jim stared at Carrie and wished he was going with them. He'd like to know that information, too!

THOUGH SHE WAS practically busting, Carrie said nothing until they reached Vanessa's Honda.

"I can't believe you said that!"

"What?" Vanessa asked, surprise on her face.

"That I had a new boyfriend!"

They got in the car before Vanessa replied. "Wasn't that why you didn't come to dinner last night?"

"No! I never said such a thing."

"You said you had other plans, didn't you?"

"Yes, but that doesn't mean a boyfriend," Carrie said, wishing she'd never said anything because now she knew what the next question would be.

"So what were your plans?"

Since finding each other again, Carrie and Vanessa

didn't keep secrets. Now Carrie wished that wasn't true. After all, the problem was Jim—and he was Vanessa's beloved big brother.

"I didn't think I should intrude on a family dinner," Carrie said stiffly, staring straight ahead.

Vanessa stared at her, not bothering to start the car. "What? But you come to family dinners all the time."

"I think I've been sponging off of your family too much, Vanessa. I never return the favor."

"Carrie, you can't expect to invite the entire family over to your apartment. Where would you put everyone?"

"I know I can't do that. But you could come over to eat once in a while."

"We had pizza at your place last week, didn't we?"

"Yes, but I didn't fix anything."

Vanessa said on a laugh, "I don't fix anything when you come over. Maybe you should invite Betty and Peter over instead of me."

Carrie gave her friend a cool look. "Maybe I should."

Vanessa turned toward her, her lips caught between her teeth, as if she was holding back the words. Finally she asked in a somber voice, "What's gotten into you? Are you trying to get rid of me?"

"No, never! You're very important to me, Vanessa, but—" She ran a trembling hand through her hair. "I don't know. Everything has changed."

"What's changed, Carrie?"

"You have a huge family now, Vanessa. You don't need me." It pained her just to say the words.

"There will always be room for you in my family no matter how big it grows, Carrie."

Her eyes filling with tears, Carrie looked out the car window. Her throat felt so tight suddenly, she couldn't speak, though Vanessa called to her.

Finally Vanessa touched her arm, and Carrie turned to her. She could see the hurt in her friend's eyes as she said, "I love having my sisters. And Jim coming home is wonderful. But none of them replaces you. The twins are both married, and I don't think Jim will be interested in hanging out with me. But you…you know me—" she gave a forced grin "—and you love me anyway. Our friendship is so important to me."

"It's important to me, too, but I don't want to feel like I'm intruding." As much as she didn't want to hurt Vanessa, Carrie knew she had to carry through her decision. There was nothing left to say except the blunt truth. "We can still do things together, but I won't be coming to any more family gatherings." She tried to discreetly wipe away her tears, but Vanessa reached out and hugged her.

Through her own tears, she said, "Whatever you say. But don't think I'm going to tell Mom. You'll have to do that yourself."

Carrie nodded. "I'll find a way to explain it."

After another hug, Vanessa started the car, and Carrie turned to face the road.

She was determined not to feel sorry for herself. It was her decision, and she felt it was the right one. She'd spent too much time in a fantasy land. It was time she ventured out into the real world.

WILL ASKED LATER, when he and Jim went to lunch, "So you and Carrie got along all right this morning?"

"We managed," Jim said, staring into his Coke. "I think I've figured out the problem. She feels threatened because I'm a man. She's afraid you won't need her anymore."

Will stared at him, and Jim, after a moment, said, "You don't think so?"

Will shook his head. "She's too smart for that. I irritate her when I try to protect her, because she's not very big. But there are a lot of things that require a woman. She knows that."

It was Jim's turn to shake his head. "I tried to compliment her twice this morning, and she turned them both back on me, accusing me of being sexist."

"That doesn't sound like Carrie. Maybe I'll ask Vanessa what's going on."

"We might know more if we knew where Carrie spent her evening last night," Jim added, not looking at Will.

Will chuckled. "Interested, are you?"

"No, of course not! I mean, Carrie is attractive, but I'm not cut out to be—to have a relationship."

"Once burned, twice shy?" Will asked.

"Not in the sense you mean. I—I fell in love with a young woman but she died in a car accident."

"Jim, I'm sorry."

Jim toyed with his spoon. "Yeah, I don't seem to bring good luck to people I love. So I'm not looking for anyone."

"Jim, surely you don't believe that. Just because one woman—"

"And everyone in my family," Jim said slowly. "That's why I wasn't sure I should contact the girls.

They all seem to be doing well." Jim cleared his throat and picked up his glass.

"You believe you're a jinx?"

"Yeah. That first night I was worried about Rebecca's baby. I'm glad everything went right for her."

"Jim, you can't be serious. You had nothing to do with your parents' death. Nor could you have been expected to take care of your brothers and sisters at your age. I don't know about the woman, but I don't think— Were you driving when—"

"No, I'd shipped out a couple of days before Lani was killed."

"Then that definitely wasn't your fault. And Wally was killed in a war. The miracle is that you came through it without a scratch."

"Not exactly without a scratch," Jim said, frowning. He still believed he had a bad effect on people he was close to, but maybe he was wrong. It just seemed that all the people he'd loved had died. That was why he was hesitant to become fond of his sisters.

"That's right. You said you were wounded," Will said.

"A couple of times," Jim muttered.

"Where were you wounded?" Will asked, letting his gaze rove over him.

"I got some shrapnel in my leg and I had a crash landing that broke my arm."

"We're glad you made it through," Will said. "But seriously, Jim, I think you need to apply some logic. You think you cause bad luck, but you don't think it was luck that you came through okay?"

"I know how to take care of myself, Will."

"So now that you're an adult, take care of those you love. That solves your problem. Right?"

"Maybe." Jim shrugged his shoulders. He wasn't going to argue with Will.

The waiter brought their orders, which, much to Jim's relief, ended that conversation.

As they ate, he mentioned the appointment he had later with the apartment manager where Carrie lived. "I thought I'd look at it before I said anything to Carrie."

"Good idea," Will said through a mouthful of BLT.

Yeah, Jim said to himself. Will thought it was a good idea...but would Carrie?

Chapter Six

"Say hello to your new neighbor!"

Carrie looked up from her desk at Will's cheerful greeting. She'd been so wrapped up in her work that she'd hardly noticed a couple of hours had passed since she'd returned from lunch with Vanessa. She gave Will a confused look. "What are you talking about?"

"Vanessa told us about the empty apartment in your building, and Jim rented it today." He clapped a rather sheepish-looking Jim on the back.

Carrie didn't move for several seconds, trying to withstand the sinking feeling deep inside her. How was she going to avoid Jim when he lived right across the hall? Still, she remembered her manners and her professionalism. "That—that's nice, Jim. When are you moving in?"

"Today," he said, staring at her.

"But it doesn't come furnished," she exclaimed, frowning.

"I can camp out until I get some furniture. It will save me a lot of money."

"I told him he should take the rest of the day off to shop, but he said he doesn't know where to go. I'm no good at that kind of stuff, Carrie. Can you show him where to find things?"

"Wouldn't Vanessa be better at that?"

"Jim will be shopping on a budget. Besides, Vanessa's never bought furniture," Will pointed out.

If she refused, Will would want to know what was wrong. She hadn't been able to explain it to Vanessa. With Will it would be even worse. "Yes, of course. I can make a list of good places for you to go to."

"Will said I could have the rest of the day off and he'll wait for the desk. Is that okay?"

"Of course. It will only take a few minutes to make the list." She picked up a pen and got out a clean sheet of paper.

"You know where I can go?"

"Yes, I know several places. There are some consignment shops in the area. Secondhand furniture is a lot cheaper than brand-new. Is that all right?"

"Probably, if it looks nice."

She nodded and started writing.

Will interrupted her. "Carrie, I think it would be better if you went with Jim. After all, he doesn't know the area like you do."

"I'm sure he'll be fine. Right, Jim?" After all, he didn't appear to want her help.

Unconvinced, Will replied, "I'd feel better about everything if you'd go with Jim, help him get set up. Is that okay with you, Jim?"

Carrie felt a sense of doom. Even Jim wouldn't deny what Will wanted.

"Sure…if you think you can spare her."

"Of course I can. It's for a good cause. You two go shop and I'll wait for the deliveries."

"Okay. Can you go now, Carrie?" Jim asked.

"Yes." She reached down for her purse and then stood. "I'm ready." What else could she do?

"Okay. Let's go. But we'll take my car so my knees aren't against the dashboard," he quickly said.

She turned to look over her shoulder. "If you prefer."

Three hours of intense shopping managed to provide Jim with a leather sofa and love seat, coffee table and end tables, two lamps, a kitchen set and a king-size bedroom suite, without mattress and box springs.

Carrie had told him he needed to buy those new.

All of them had been purchased at low prices because they'd been gently used before.

"Wow!" Jim said as they got back in his car. "That's incredible. And it didn't cost nearly as much as I thought it would."

"Do you think you're through?"

He looked at her in surprise. "There's more?"

"You have no dishes, silverware, pots and pans, sheets or towels. I'm afraid they're all necessary. We can go to Target and get all those things…if you want." She was offering him a way out, because she didn't think he'd want her assistance.

"Yeah, I'm ready. With you for a guide, we'll be through in no time."

"Am I pushing you into making decisions? If it's too fast, we can quit for tonight."

"No, I definitely want to go on, but I do need to eat

some dinner. How about you join me? That's the least I can do for all your time. Then afterward, we can go on with our shopping."

"Oh, no, that's not necessary. I—"

"Don't tell me you've already made plans. I haven't given you any time to make plans," he said, leaning down to see her face since she'd ducked her head.

"I was just going to say that—that there's no need to buy me dinner because…"

"You've given up food for Lent? No, it's not spring, so that can't be it. You're like a camel and can go without food for days at a time?"

"Don't be ridiculous, Jim!" she snapped.

He waited until they were in his car. "I'm going to get Vanessa to go over to my apartment and wait for the deliveries. It's great that they can deliver this evening, isn't it?"

"Yes, as long as you pay extra."

He grinned. "I've saved so much money, that's not a problem. In the meantime, I owe you dinner. And I always pay my debts."

Carrie was too tired to argue with his firm statement. After he got Vanessa on the phone, he drove both of them to a small Italian restaurant. "I hope you like Italian," he murmured.

"Yes, I do. And this is a lovely restaurant."

"Good."

Once they were seated and had ordered, she said, "Vanessa was okay with waiting for your deliveries?"

"Yeah. Makes me feel humble, though. She was happy to do something for me." He shook his head.

"I've come back into her life after twenty-some-odd years and she thinks it's an honor to help me out."

"It is. Vanessa loves the feel of family around her."

"She's always had family," Jim pointed out.

"You never met Vivian's husband."

"You don't mean Will, do you?"

"No, Herbert. He was extremely old-fashioned and domineering. I don't know how Vivian managed to live with him as long as she did." Carrie shivered. Her father hadn't had a clue as far as finances went, but he wasn't cold and domineering like Herbert Shaw.

"Not like Vivian, I gather," Jim said wryly, watching her.

"No. They were opposites."

The waiter brought their food. After he left the table, Jim said, "It's funny how opposites attract. I had several guys under me marry women who were as different from them as night from day."

Carrie said, "But you only heard one side of the marriage, right? So you don't know if that was accurate or not."

"True. And I didn't have any desire to investigate," he said with a grin. "In spite of their complaints, they seemed happier after marriage than they did before."

"And that fact didn't tempt you to marry?"

Jim stiffened in his chair. "No. No, that didn't tempt me. A soldier's life is hard on women."

"Unless she's a soldier, too?"

"Don't try to accuse me of being sexist again, Carrie." After a moment, he added, "I've worked with women soldiers in certain situations and they did a great job."

"Good. But I would think a marriage between two soldiers would double the problems in a marriage."

"Yeah."

They ate for several minutes without talking.

Finally Jim said, "I'm sorry if I made you feel uncomfortable today."

Carrie tensed. Then she drew a deep breath. "Don't worry. Tomorrow you'll have your own desk and your computer should be there soon after we open the office."

"Good. I'll have to set up my desk, too."

"Yes, and then everything will go back to normal."

After studying her silently, he said, "What's normal?"

She shrugged her shoulders. "Everyone working. We haven't gotten a lot done, what with your arrival and Jamie's birth."

"Right. The faster I pick things up, the better off we'll be. I think I can do a lot right away."

"And you'll want to schedule a meeting with Mr. Michaels. He needs to be reassured."

"Have you worked with him before?"

"Yes," Carrie said, dropping her gaze to her plate. Why tell Jim that Mr. Michaels's cases were the easy ones? They still needed to be done.

"Is there something you're not telling me?"

He was too perceptive for his own good. "There's a lot I'm not telling you, Jim. I can't explain everything we've done for the past five years. Some things you'll have to find out for yourself."

"Okay, I'm a believer of that philosophy. I think you learn more by doing than listening."

They finished their meal and returned to the car,

where Jim asked for instructions to find the nearest Target. Carrie gave him the information and then sat back, allowing him to be in charge. It had been a long day and she was tired.

It was a full two hours later when they finally returned to the apartments. Lugging packages, they walked up to the second floor, to the apartment opposite Carrie's. Jim knocked on his door and Vanessa opened it.

"Oh, Jim, the furniture is beautiful! You did a great job. And so fast!" Vanessa said, drawing her brother and Carrie into the apartment. "I arranged it, but you can change it however you want it."

Jim stood there surveying the furniture he'd bought. "It looks great the way it is. Good job, Vanessa," he said, stooping to kiss her cheek. "Now, you and Carrie can start unpacking while I go bring up the rest of our purchases."

He disappeared before Carrie could object.

"What all did you buy?" Vanessa asked, eagerly reaching for one of the sacks.

"Everything he needs for an apartment. At least I hope so." She opened a box of dishes, setting out a service for four in cobalt-blue.

"I like that color," Vanessa said as she opened the pots and pans.

"So did Jim. Amazing you'd have the same taste, isn't it?"

"I guess so. But I can't believe he managed to buy so much in such a short space of time. I know I couldn't do that."

Carrie shrugged her shoulders. "Maybe you could if I was helping you—and you didn't have a place until you did."

Vanessa looked at Carrie with a questioning look. "Are you okay?"

Carrie gave her friend a hug. "Yes, I'm just tired."

"Sit down while I unpack. It's like Christmas, isn't it?" Vanessa enthused as she returned to the table where the bags had been dropped. Just then the door opened again and Jim returned with more boxes and packages.

"This is it," he announced, taking deep breaths. "Those stairs are going to keep me in shape." After a quick glance at Carrie, he added, "Like your friend there."

Carrie ignored the implied compliment. "I'm glad we were able to do so much, but if you don't mind, I'm going to bed now. It's been a long day." With a nod she slipped from the room.

Vanessa looked at her brother. "Did you do something to Carrie?"

"Nothing more than wear her out trying to find everything I need."

"Except a mattress. Where are you going to sleep?"

"Tonight on the sofa. I'll get a mattress tomorrow."

"But you haven't even bought any food. How will you manage breakfast in the morning? Promise you'll come to our house for breakfast. Please?"

"Okay, if you're sure Betty won't mind."

"You could come spend the night, too. It would save your trying to make sense of all this tonight."

"No, Vanessa, I'm staying here tonight, but I'll be over in the morning. What time?"

"Eight-thirty? You could bring Carrie, too. She hasn't come to breakfast in a while."

"I'm not sure she'll come, but I'll try," he promised and hugged his sister good-bye. "I'll see you in the morning."

CARRIE WAS UP at her usual time the next morning. She'd had no trouble going to sleep last night. This morning, after stretching, she almost felt normal.

Until she remembered that Jim was just across the hall. She thought she'd had herself under control. Until yesterday. She'd gotten way too involved in his life. But that was over, she vowed. He had what he needed.

Jim was all set up in a nice apartment, albeit in the wrong place, with everything he needed. Today things would return to normal.

A knock on the door startled her. She put down the skim milk she was drinking and walked over to peer through the peephole.

Swinging open the door, she tried for a pleasant tone. "Good morning."

"Morning," Jim replied, adding a lazy smile. "Vanessa invited us both over for breakfast this morning. I didn't know how early you'd be up, so I—"

"Thanks, but I just finished my breakfast."

He looked over her shoulder, as if trying to verify her words. "A glass of milk?"

"I have skim milk in the morning along with toast." Then Carrie got angry with herself for giving him those details.

"Come with me. You've got room for a little more breakfast, and Vanessa will be disappointed if you're not there."

"No, she won't, as long as you're there," Carrie snapped.

Jim's eyes narrowed. "Is that what's wrong? Are you jealous of the attention Vanessa's been showing me?"

Carrie drew a deep breath. "No, I'm not jealous at all. I'm thrilled for Vanessa that you've finally come home. But I have already had my breakfast and I'm going to work."

"You'll be the only one there. Will will be having breakfast with all of us. He'll be expecting you, too."

"He'll survive. Thank you for stopping by. I'll see you at the office." She started closing the door, thinking she'd ended the conversation.

Jim put his foot in the door, stopping her. "You're going to upset everyone if you don't come. Is that what you want? To create a stir?"

Carrie dropped her head. She couldn't win! "No, that's not what I want," she muttered in a low voice, "but—"

"Come and have a cup of coffee at least. You can slip out early if you think it's necessary."

His suggestion made sense, but she hated going along with him. After a moment of silent debate, she lifted her chin. "Fine, I'll come for a few minutes. Then I'll go on to the office."

"Good. Want to share a car?"

"How would I go to the office early if we only have one car?"

"I could come later with Will."

"Fine. Let me get my purse."

Jim stood there, his face showing no emotion. What did he have to frown about? He'd won the argument, Carrie reminded herself.

After getting her purse and keys, she locked her door and led the way down the stairs. When they reached the parking lot, she headed to her own car.

"Wait a minute," Jim called. "Let's take my rental car."

"No, I have to have my car if I'm going to leave for the office before you do." She opened the door and slid behind the wheel, waiting for him to follow.

Jim crawled into the passenger seat with a frown on his face. "I don't know why you couldn't drive my car to the office."

"Because I'm not listed as a driver on your rental. If something happened, your insurance wouldn't pay."

"I need to get my own car," he muttered.

"Probably. Will knows a lot about the local dealers. He can help you." She didn't want him involving her in that process. She was going to work today.

He was more perceptive than she'd thought. "So I've worn out your generosity with all our shopping yesterday?"

"No, I didn't mean that. I just thought you should use Will's experience."

Nothing more was said until they reached the Green-field house. When she got out of her car, Jim had already circled the vehicle to help her out. As they walked to the door, he put his hand on her back, a typical male gesture to guide the woman in his charge.

Only she wasn't in his care. She was independent. She sped up to put some distance between them.

"What's wrong?" he asked, catching up to her as she waited for the front door to open.

She pretended she didn't know what he was talking about. Giving him a quizzical look over her shoulder, she swung back around as Peter, Betty's husband, answered the door.

"Good morning, Peter. I hope you're expecting us," she said, smiling at the man.

"'Course we are, Miss Carrie. Come right in. They're all at the table already, but there's plenty left for the two of you."

"I'm sure," Carrie said. "With Betty cooking, there's always plenty of food."

Jim offered Peter his hand. Then he followed Carrie to the dining room.

Will stood as they came in. "We're glad you made it. Vanessa was getting antsy. She kept wanting to call both of you, but I told her you'd get here." He beamed at both of them.

Carrie took a deep breath, hiding her relief that she'd decided to come. It was so easy to fall into the warm embrace of this loving family. She'd have to be careful.

"I had to twist Carrie's arm," Jim drawled, and Carrie wanted to stomp on his toes. "She thought she needed to be at the office early today."

"We don't have anything early today, do we, honey?" Will asked, looking at her.

"No, of course not, but I didn't get much work done yesterday."

"She spent all her time helping me get set up," Jim pointed out.

Vanessa spoke. "You'd be amazed, Mom. They managed to do so much in one day."

"I can't wait to see. What do you want for a housewarming gift, Jim?" Vivian asked, taking Jim by surprise.

"Uh, nothing. That's not necessary."

"He doesn't have a coffeemaker yet, Vivian," Carrie said, avoiding Jim's gaze.

"Wonderful, Carrie. We'll get you that, Jim. Do you prefer a certain kind?"

"No. But really, Vivian, that's not necessary."

Will stopped the argument. "You might as well graciously accept, Jim. Vivian won't be deterred. Here, have some eggs," Will said, passing a platter.

Betty entered at that moment. "Don't you be offering him those cold eggs! I have some hot ones right here," she assured Will. She immediately circled the table to serve both Carrie and Jim.

Carrie just took a spoonful, determined to eat and get out as quickly as possible. When Jim did the same, Betty spooned more onto his plate. Carrie couldn't hold back a smile.

Next Peter entered the room with warm cinnamon rolls. Carrie's mouth watered just from their aroma. She took one, bit it and closed her eyes to enjoy its sweet flavor.

Jim leaned over and whispered, "Glad you came?"

Her eyes popped open and she glared at him. "Of course, but my hips aren't."

She felt the heat from Jim's eyes scorch her skin as

they made their way down from her face over her neck, where her pulse beat suddenly faster. They lingered on the curves of her breasts and finally landed on her hips. By the time he raised his head to her, she felt as if she'd spontaneously combust. Then, leaning in close, so close she could smell the musk of his aftershave, he whispered in a husky voice, "I don't see a problem."

Carrie nearly choked on her cinnamon roll. Problem? Her pulse still raced. They had a problem, all right.

Chapter Seven

When Carrie excused herself and left, Jim looked at Will. "Do you mind giving me a ride to work?"

"Of course I will. You still have the rental?"

"Yeah, but I need to buy a car. Carrie said you knew most of the dealerships in the area."

"Sure. What kind of car are you looking for?"

"Ooh, get a convertible," Vanessa suggested.

Jim smiled at his baby sister. "I don't think convertibles are safe, honey. You don't drive one, do you?"

"No, but—"

"I was thinking about some kind of SUV," Jim said to Vanessa, but he also gave Will a look. "I need something where my knees aren't pressed up against the dashboard like they are in Carrie's car."

"I agree," Will said. "We can look today if you want. Unless Carrie has something I need to do this morning."

"I'd like that…after you check with Carrie," Jim said, hoping Will would take the hint. He didn't want to be responsible for making Will unavailable if Carrie needed him.

"I'll check with her right now. Are you almost ready to leave?"

"Sure. I've done about all the damage I can do this morning," he said, patting his stomach. As Betty came in, he added, "Betty, this was the best breakfast I've ever had. Thanks a lot."

Betty beamed. "Happens every morning, Jim."

Then Jim stood and thanked Vivian for making him feel so welcome.

"You're family, Jim. You're always welcome," Vivian said with a warm smile.

Vanessa stood and hugged his arm. "Mom's right, you know."

Will came in and joined his wife, giving her a good-bye kiss. Then he turned to Jim. "Ready?"

It was after they'd gotten into the car that Will asked Jim, "You and Carrie still cross with each other?"

"Why would you think that?" Jim replied, staring straight ahead.

"I'm guessing you rode with Carrie because you weren't sure she'd come if you didn't."

Jim smiled. "You're good, Will. She was reluctant to come with me this morning. Somehow it seemed important that she join us."

"Well, let's get this car thing settled. I'll follow you to take back your rental. Then we'll hit a couple of dealerships and see what they've got. Will you need to get a loan?"

"No. I've saved most of my salary since I entered the Marines at the age of eighteen. Plus my combat pay."

Even though it was only days ago since he'd been in

the marines, wearing his uniform and taking orders, it suddenly seemed like a lifetime ago.

He could easily imagine himself leading this new life, with his sisters, with Will and Vivian...with Carrie.

Where did that thought come from?

Living under the curse he'd endured since childhood, Jim knew there could never be anything between him and Carrie. He'd best remember that, no matter how attracted to her he was.

CARRIE WAS WORKING at her computer when the two men finally reached the office. She automatically checked her watch. Since it was already two in the afternoon, they had less than half a day to work. But, of course, she certainly wasn't going to mention their absence.

After greeting them with a smile, she turned back to her computer.

"Aren't you going to ask us what we were doing?" Will prompted.

Recognizing he wanted her to do so, she said, "Of course, Will. What have you been doing?"

"We've been buying Jim a car!"

"Really? What did you buy, Jim?"

"An SUV. It takes a lot of room for someone as tall as me."

"That's wonderful." Again she turned back to her computer.

"If you don't mind, I'll need to catch a ride home this afternoon. I can't pick it up until morning." Jim stood beside her desk, almost—in her mind—daring her to say no.

But she wouldn't fall into that trap. "Yes, of course."

He didn't go away.

She looked up again. "Was there something else?"

Jim rubbed the back of his neck, looking rather sheepish. "Well, yeah. I hate to ask because you've done so much for me but…"

"What is it, Jim?" she asked impatiently.

"I need to go grocery shopping this evening after work."

Carrie didn't know whether to cry. She'd spent countless hours identifying her problem. She had a stupid crush on Jim. Then she'd spent sleepless nights deciding she had to pull away from him, not spend any time with him. But after all that, he was making it impossible.

"I can take you shopping," she finally said.

"Good, because I'll admit I haven't done much grocery shopping in my life. Soldiers don't do their own cooking." He flashed her one of his smiles that made her want to melt at his feet.

Stiffening her back, she gave him an abrupt nod and turned back to the computer. As she did so, to forestall any more requests, she said, "You need to get your desk set up with the new supplies. I'll put away whatever is left over when you're finished."

"Okay, sure. Thanks, Carrie," he added.

Out of the corner of her eye, she noted he was still smiling, and she ground her teeth.

Since the men were in the office for the rest of the afternoon, Carrie abruptly decided to return to the Riley residence. She had discovered Richard's brother, Charles, was a hundred-and-fifty-pound weakling, totally incapable of lifting his brother. She hoped to stake out the Riley house for an hour or two and see if she could get any pictures of Richard Riley out of his wheelchair.

She stood and picked up her purse. Then she went to the door of Will's office. "I'm going out to check on one of our cases. I'll be back around five."

"Okay," he agreed, scarcely looking up. But he had second thoughts before she could escape. "Which case?"

"Well, there are several cases I'm taking with me." That was true. She was going to update other files while she watched the Riley house.

"You're going to the Riley house, aren't you?" Will asked, standing and coming toward her.

"Will, I'm only going to watch. I'm not going to confront him."

"If he catches you taking pictures of him, there will be a confrontation whether you want it or not. Jim, could you go with Carrie? I would, but I've got a call I'm waiting for."

"Will, no! I don't need—"

"Sure, I'll be glad to. Wish I had my SUV, though."

"Take my car. Carrie used hers last time. They may have noticed it."

"There's no need for me to go if Jim is going. It doesn't take two people to do a stakeout," Carrie said stiffly. She couldn't believe Will was suddenly treating her like a little girl.

"If it was one of the normal cases, I wouldn't send Jim with you. But this one is special. There's a lot of money at risk and that man is...evil."

"I'll be fine, Will."

"I need you to do this, Carrie. I promised Vivian I

wouldn't let you get hurt." Will stood there, pleading with his eyes.

She hated when he did that.

"Fine! Prepare to be bored, Jim! And we're taking *my* car." She stomped out of the office.

JIM HURRIED after Carrie. If he hadn't caught up to her before she reached her car, he figured she'd drive off without him.

Instead, he managed to plant his knees against the dashboard and buckle up before Carrie started the car.

She gave him a hard look. "Comfortable?"

He knew it wasn't concern in her voice. "Hey, Carrie, Will only wanted me to go because of Riley. You know he'd soon as shoot you as look at you. It won't hurt to have an extra pair of eyes along."

She said nothing as she backed out of the parking lot and pulled into traffic. In fact, she said nothing for the next ten minutes.

Jim watched her. She was an unusual woman. She never wasted energy and always appeared in complete control. She would've made a good soldier except for one thing. She had a rebellious streak. He could handle it. But what bothered him more than anything was the protective streak he'd discovered he had for Carrie. He had to constantly remind himself that she wasn't his business.

"If you don't stop frowning, you're going to look about twenty years older," he said softly, watching her reaction.

If anything, she frowned more fiercely.

"I suppose if I suggested you smile, you'd growl?"

She stopped at a red light and turned to face him. "If your competency was being challenged, would you be smiling?"

"Carrie, both Will and I explained it's not your competency that's in question. It's just that this particular man is difficult."

"Most fraud criminals are difficult, Jim. And I've been chasing them down for years. Suddenly I can't go out alone?"

"Maybe Will is just trying to get his money's worth out of me," Jim suggested solemnly.

"I don't think babysitting is good usage of your time."

"Come on, Carrie. You know Will respects your skills and trusts you. You have to admit that." He paused, but Carrie said nothing. "Look at it this way," he continued, "I'll keep you amused by telling you war stories while we wait."

She sighed and shrugged her shoulders. "I guess that's an offer I can't refuse."

"Good girl!" he said. When she glared at him, he immediately changed his words to "Good, uh, woman?"

She gave him a cool look. "Good boy."

"Hey! I corrected myself." He didn't mind her teasing him. At least she wasn't mad anymore.

Instead of responding, she pulled to the side of the road on the quiet street where the Rileys lived, parking in a tight spot behind another car.

"I'm rethinking my choice of an SUV," Jim murmured. "I'm not sure it will do well in undercover work."

"Don't worry, Jim. I'll be glad to loan you my car," Carrie said sweetly.

Jim grinned. "Yeah, I just bet you would."

After a moment of silence, Jim asked the obvious question. "So we just sit here and wait for them to appear?"

"That's basically it. Real dangerous, huh?"

"Could be, honey."

"Don't call me honey!" she snapped.

Jim gave her a calm look. "You know, when I was in Iraq, things looked calm like this. Then we'd get a suicide bomber, or snipers would begin firing. If we let ourselves get lulled into even a moment of inattention, someone would pay."

Carrie shuddered at his words. "That must've made for a very tense time."

"Yeah." He had offered to tell her war stories, but he was having a hard time doing that. There were too many tragic stories that he didn't want to remember. He'd lost some good friends to enemy fire.

"Why did you stay in the marines for such a long time?"

He pondered her question, then finally said, "I didn't have anywhere to go or anything in particular to do."

"Until Will found you?"

"Yeah. I wanted to see my little sisters again before—before anything happened."

"You expected to die?" Carrie asked, her voice rising in protest.

"Why not? My brother died. Many of my friends died. Why not me?" he asked, voicing the question he'd asked himself many times. Sure, he'd been vigilant. But so had others.

After a moment of silence, Carrie said in a low voice, "I'm glad you came home."

"Me, too," Jim agreed, trying to keep any emotion from his voice. But he couldn't help remembering those hot days in the desert when he'd dreamed of sitting in a car on a cool afternoon with a blonde beside him. Of course, he hadn't intended it to be a stakeout.

Then he thought about Lani, the woman he'd planned on marrying. She'd been so sweet. Before he'd left for his next tour of duty, they'd made plans. Plans that had disintegrated when she died in a car accident two days after his departure. He hadn't been able to return in time for her funeral. That had been eight years ago.

That was when he'd realized he had no business involving a woman in his life again. He had to remember that. He was already allowing Carrie to occupy too much of his thoughts.

Too bad.

Suddenly Carrie stilled, her gaze focused on the house halfway down the block. "They're leaving," she whispered as if the Rileys could hear her. She blindly reached for the camera she'd put beside her at the ready.

Jim narrowed his gaze, wishing he had binoculars, but he supposed their adversaries might notice that.

"Damn!" Carrie muttered as a floral delivery truck rolled to a stop a few houses away. "They're shielded from us by that truck."

"Want me to take a stroll down the street?" Jim offered.

"No, we don't take chances. Besides, you're rather noticeable, Jim."

"Why?"

She rolled her eyes. "You're tall, handsome. His wife would notice you even if he didn't. We stay in the car and live to fight another day."

"Are you sure I'll be any good at this work?"

"Yes, you'll do well. Just learn not to take chances." While she talked, she snapped some pictures of Richard Riley, his wife and brother gathered by the side of a green van, but the pictures were through the tinted windows of the vehicle.

"Can you see anything?"

Carrie continued to snap photos. "Not really, but maybe when we enlarge them we'll be surprised."

After the Rileys' vehicle drove away, Carrie put away her camera and started her car.

"What now?" Jim asked.

"We go back to the office and upload the pictures."

Jim rode quietly beside Carrie. He was actually learning a lot by accompanying Carrie as she did her job. Will had emphasized that they didn't take chances, but Carrie was demonstrating how she did her job in those circumstances.

When they got back to the office, Will met them in the outer office. He must've heard their footsteps before they reached the door.

"You're back early. Is everything okay?" he asked, his gaze flicking back and forth between the two of them.

"Of course," Carrie said, using an offhand manner to convince Will.

Jim concurred. "Carrie followed orders, keeping a low profile and taking no chances, in spite of my offering to chase them down."

Will shot her a grin. "Good girl."

"Careful," Jim warned. "I was called to order on that comment."

"What do you mean?" Will asked.

Carrie ignored them both as Jim brought Will up to speed. She settled in at her desk till Will, in a duly penitent voice, called out, "Like I should've said, 'Good job, Carrie!'"

"Thank you," she said coolly. "Too bad Jim didn't stay here and get some work done, instead of wasting his time keeping me company."

Jim stood stiffly beside Carrie's desk. "I didn't waste my time. I learned quite a bit by working with you."

"Go learn from Will!" Carrie snapped. "I'm busy!"

WHAT WAS WRONG with the man? How dare he try to get on her good side by flattering her? She was trying so hard to keep her distance. It was so tempting to believe that he meant those casual words. But she wasn't that gullible.

For the next hour she worked hard to concentrate on her job. Unfortunately none of the shots she'd taken at the Riley's had proven helpful. Instead, she worked on other cases for the insurance companies.

Jim, after going into Will's office for a few minutes, came back out and began organizing his desk. Even though he was ignoring her, he was distracting. Today he was wearing khaki pants and a knit shirt that hugged his broad chest and drew attention to his brown eyes. His dark hair framed a strong face, with dark brows.

Carrie sighed. She didn't need to look at him. From all the time she'd stared at his picture on her desk—the picture she'd safely stored away days ago—she knew exactly what he looked like. His handsome image was branded on her mind.

As she worked on the computer, she could hear Jim moving around, his well-conditioned body doing so effortlessly.

It made her picture his body. Stop it! she ordered herself, but she couldn't get him out of her mind. He'd lived there too long before he even came home. Somehow, her dream Jim had filled in all the lonely parts of her life, and it was hard to keep him out now.

When it was almost five, she began putting things away. She'd fought the good fight long enough. She could only hope he'd go out on his own frequently.

Or maybe he'd decide this job wasn't for him.

No, she couldn't hope that. It would be devastating if Jim went away. But maybe it would be better than dying a slow death watching him find someone to love and marry.

She cleared her desk as she debated her choices.

"Is it time to leave, Carrie?" Jim asked.

"I thought we'd wrap things up, since we still have to do your grocery shopping."

"Oh, yeah. I'd almost forgotten." Jim hurriedly cleared his desk and stood, walking to Will's office.

"We're getting ready to go, Will. Carrie is going to take me grocery shopping."

"I'm ready to go, too." As he stood, Will added, "When I talked to Vivian a little while ago, she said there was a front moving in. A big storm is supposed to hit in an hour or so. Could be rain."

Jim frowned. "This is Dallas. I thought it was always warm here in late October."

Carrie smiled but said nothing.

"Wrong, Jim. In Dallas, the weather frequently changes. You have a jacket?"

"Not really. I have to shop for that, too." He turned to Carrie. "Did you hear what Will said about the weather?"

"Yes."

"Do you want to skip the grocery shopping until the weather is better?" he asked in concern.

"Don't be silly, Jim. I don't melt just because it's raining. Besides, we might finish our shopping before the storm gets here. Ready?"

"Yeah. We're going, Will."

Will came out of his office. "You two could come to dinner at the house and shop another day."

"No, we're going to get it done tonight. Thanks, anyway," Carrie said briskly. She didn't want any future evenings spent with Jim. That would be too much.

When they reached the parking lot, Carrie automatically looked at the sky. There were storm clouds gathering in the northwest. She walked faster.

Once she and Jim were in her car, she told him they were going to the grocery store closest to their apartments.

"Is there something in particular you're looking for?"

He gave her a surprised look. "No, not at all. I'm a beginning cook. Maybe you could help me learn a few tricks," he said, looking at her expectantly.

She swallowed hard and looked away. "Actually, I believe in going to an expert when I want to learn something. I suggest you ask Betty for cooking tips."

"Good idea," Jim said, as if pleased with her suggestion.

Breathing a sigh of relief, she pulled her car into the grocery store parking lot.

The next half hour was more fun than Carrie expected. While shopping, Jim teased her about her taste for boxed macaroni and cheese, and peas. He'd had enough of them in the military to last a lifetime. She couldn't help but laugh when he shared some of the horror stories from the mess hall.

When they came out of the grocery store, each carrying two bags of groceries, they discovered the temperature had dropped drastically and the storm clouds had come closer.

"We'd better hurry," Carrie urged.

They stored the bags in the hatchback and jumped in the car. Carrie took the shortest route home.

Just as they got there, the clouds opened up and the rain poured down.

"Run on in, Carrie. I'll bring the bags," Jim ordered, assuming she'd do as he said.

"Don't be ridiculous. If we each take two bags, there won't be a need for a second trip." She looked outside the window at the driving rain. "But we'll need to hurry."

"Okay, if you're sure."

They got out of the car and ran to the back of it, each gathering up the paper bags. Then they raced to the shelter of the apartment hallway.

When they reached safety from the storm, they skidded into each other, both laughing at their antics. Water was dripping off their hair onto their faces as they grinned at each other.

Suddenly Jim stopped laughing and stepped closer, lowering his head to Carrie's for a kiss, inch by tantalizing inch.

Chapter Eight

Everything went into slow motion as Carrie stood there, mesmerized by Jim's chocolate-brown eyes. She could feel his breath on her face, smell his musky scent, and her heart leapt in anticipation of his lips on hers. She already knew what they would feel like. Hadn't she dreamed of his kisses for over a year?

Jim was a hairsbreadth away from her mouth when she suddenly realized what she was about to do. Kiss Jim Barlow? That was exactly what she wasn't supposed to do. At the last minute, she pulled back and stammered, "W-we'd better get these groceries up to your apartment before they spoil."

With that she spun away from him and raced up the flight of stairs. She heard Jim follow a few moments later, leaving her to wait by his door, her heart pounding not from her run up the steps but from their near-kiss.

When Jim came up alongside her to unlock the door, she sidestepped him and then zipped inside the open door, setting her bags on the kitchen counter. Then she hurried back to the door, skirting around Jim as he entered.

"Well, good luck. I'll see you tomorrow," she said hastily as she exited the apartment.

"Carrie!" Jim called in protest, but she ignored him. She was heading for safety to her own apartment with the door locked behind her. No more temptation tonight. She'd almost made a big mistake, and she wasn't taking any more risks.

"DAMN!" JIM MUTTERED under his breath as he stood, his hands on his hips, in his empty kitchen. He hadn't intended to— No, he had to be honest. He had wanted to kiss Carrie. She'd looked so cute with rain dripping off her hair, her eyes shining, a big smile on those lips. Yeah, he'd wanted to taste them. To feel her warmth against him.

What was wrong with him? He'd told himself that he shouldn't fall for another woman. It would only cause heartache and pain. Who knew what would happen if he let himself fall for Carrie?

He couldn't do that to her.

Sighing, he began putting away his groceries. Maybe he'd been too long without a woman. Yeah, that was it. It couldn't have anything to do with Carrie's beauty, her intelligence, her strengths. No, nothing to do with those things.

With a wry laugh, he paused in his activity. Okay, so now that he'd been honest with himself, what was he going to do about it? He couldn't pursue her. Not after she'd indicated she didn't want anything to do with him. She was his sister's best friend. He was going to have to be around her. Hell, he'd even arranged to work with her.

Talk about making a mess of things!

Should he tell Will he didn't want the job? But he did. It seemed to him the job was suited to his particular skills. He felt comfortable with Will. He didn't want to walk away.

He didn't want to leave Carrie.

Whoa! That was one of those thoughts he needed to bury deep within him. His future might lie with Will and Carrie for work, but not personally. He needed to keep that in mind.

AT THE OFFICE the next morning, everything seemed to have calmed down, much to Carrie's relief. She'd made sure she'd left the apartment before Jim could ask for any favors. She thought it was strange that neither he nor Will had come to the office, but she was sure they were both busy.

As she was determined to be.

She was so successful, she almost didn't notice the men's footsteps until they reached the office. She looked up, a smile on her lips. "Good morning."

"Hi, Carrie," Will called out cheerfully. "Come see Jim's new car!"

"Oh! I forgot— Was I supposed to drop you off to pick it up? I didn't think—"

"It's okay, Carrie," Jim responded. "Will volunteered to drive me."

"Wait until you see it, Carrie. It's great. I'm thinking of getting one just like it," Will said.

"Will Vivian like that?" She couldn't quite picture the delicate and elegant Vivian climbing into an SUV.

Will grinned wryly. "Probably not. But you'll like it. Come see."

She couldn't refuse Will's enthusiastic invitation, unless she wanted to look like a sourpuss. So she followed them down the stairs to the parking lot, where Jim had parked his new blue SUV. He unlocked it and insisted Carrie get behind the wheel.

"Jim, I'll never be driving it. Why should I—"

"You never know, Carrie," Will said. "Jim could borrow your car for surveillance and you'd have to drive his. But it wouldn't be a problem for you. See? You're a perfect fit."

"It's very nice, Jim," she assured him as she slid down from the high-profile vehicle. "Now I'd better get back to work."

Will shot Jim a puzzled look. "Did something happen last night?" he asked when Carrie had left them.

"What do you mean?" Jim replied, his gaze fastened on the door through which Carrie had disappeared.

"Come on, man, you know what I mean. Did you and Carrie have another argument?"

Jim turned to look at Will, pulling his thoughts together. "No, not at all. In fact, our grocery shopping was quite successful." Then, crossing his fingers that he'd manage to distract Will, he said, "She suggested I ask Betty for cooking lessons. What do you think?"

"Good idea. Betty will like that."

"Oh, terrific. Well, as Carrie said, we'd better get to work. My week is almost up. I'd like to have something to show for it."

"VIV, IS VANESSA THERE?" Will asked when his wife answered the phone.

"Why, yes, she is. Why?"

"I need to ask her something."

As soon as her mother passed the phone to her, Vanessa asked, "Hello, Will. What's up?"

"Honey, have you talked to Carrie lately?"

"Sure. I saw her night before last when she and Jim got in from shopping. It was like Christmas, they had so many packages." She chuckled.

"Did you talk to her alone?"

"Not really. Why? Is something wrong?" Vanessa asked, alarm rising.

"I don't know. But she hasn't seemed the same since Jim got here. I want him to work with us, but...I owe my loyalty to Carrie. Can you try to find out what's going on?"

"Sure. I'll ask her to lunch today. Is that all right?"

"That would be great."

After hanging up the phone, Vanessa turned a puzzled face to her mother. "Will is concerned that there's something going on between Jim and Carrie."

"Did he indicate anything in particular?"

Vanessa frowned. "He said Carrie hadn't been the same since Jim got here. He wants them all to work well together, but..."

"And I thought my husband was a smart man," Vivian said with a laugh.

"What, Mom? What do you mean?"

"Have you looked at your brother lately?"

"Well, of course I have. He's so handsome— You're saying Carrie is attracted to him?"

"Is she alive?" Vivian drawled. "Any red-blooded American woman would be."

"But that would be perfect!" Vanessa exclaimed. "Then Carrie would really be part of the family!"

"That would certainly be a happy ending. But are you sure Carrie would risk that ending?"

"What do you mean, Mom? Why not?"

"Because if she misjudged Jim's response, what would happen? They would have to work together. Spend their free time together if they were associating with the family. Carrie could lose everything if she fell for Jim and he didn't fall for her."

"What are we going to do? I don't want to lose Carrie again. Or Jim, either."

Vivian patted her daughter's shoulder. "Of course not. Here's what you need to do."

CARRIE ANSWERED the phone. "Greenfield and Associates."

"Carrie, it's Vanessa. Do you have time for lunch today?"

"Not really, Vanessa. I'm in the middle of something. How about next week?"

"It's important, Carrie. Can't you work me in today?"

Not wanting to disappoint her friend, Carrie said, "Okay, but we have to make it quick."

"Great! I'll see you at eleven-thirty."

Carrie hung up the phone, puzzlement on her face. What was so important that Vanessa just had to see her?

"Anything wrong?" Jim asked from his desk.

Carrie jerked her head up and looked at him. "No. Nothing is wrong."

Will came out of his office, having just gotten off the other line. "Was that Ned Browning? I've been waiting for him to call."

"No, it was Vanessa. She wants me to go to lunch."

Will turned to Jim. "I guess we'll go when you get back. That okay with you?"

"Sure. I ate breakfast this morning. There's no hurry."

"Did you cook it yourself?" Will asked with a grin.

Jim returned the laugh and went along with the joke. "Absolutely. I boiled an egg and made toast. I'm a fast learner."

"Carrie taught you that?"

"No, I figured it out on my own," Jim immediately said, but his gaze shifted to Carrie.

Quickly she looked down at the papers on her desk. It was important that she not be involved in Jim's personal life. It was bad enough that she had to work with him every day.

The phone rang again. This time it was the call Will was waiting for.

"Thanks, Carrie. I'll take it in my office." He entered his office and closed the door.

"Who is Browning?" Jim asked.

"He's head of security for Global Life," she said as she turned back toward her computer.

Before she could actually get started, Jim asked, "Have I done something wrong?"

Carrie spun back around and stared at him. "No! I

mean, I didn't see you this morning so, of course, you didn't."

"And last night?"

"No. We both got a little wet, but I dried out just fine. Nothing to worry about," she insisted, but she avoided looking at him.

"Guess I just imagined it," Jim said.

Carrie risked a quick glance at his handsome face. Then she buried her nose in her work and didn't look up until Vanessa arrived.

"Big brother!" she exclaimed, and hugged Jim's neck as he stood to greet her.

"Hi, Vanessa. How are you?"

"I'm fine. I just visited Rebecca and little Jamie. She wants to know when you're going to pay them a call."

"I've had a lot to get settled, but I plan on dropping by soon."

"Good. That's what I told her." Vanessa smiled at Jim and turned to Carrie. "Are you ready for lunch?"

"Let me just shut down my computer, and I'll be ready," Carrie said as she closed the file she'd been working on. Then she shut down the computer and stood.

"I'll be back in an hour," she said to Jim. Without waiting for a reply, she strode out of the office, but not before seeing Vanessa look over her shoulder and wink at her brother on her way out.

"How's everything going?" Vanessa asked casually after they ordered.

"Fine. Everything's fine."

"Good. I'm so thrilled that Jim is here."

"Maybe you should've asked *him* to lunch instead of me." Carrie regretted her words as soon as she heard them, but it was too late to take them back.

"Carrie, is something wrong?"

"No. I mean—everyone keeps asking me what's wrong. Nothing's wrong. I'm just trying to do my job."

"And I'm sure you're doing a good job. Will always has high praise for your work," Vanessa said soothingly.

Carrie drew a deep breath. "I'm sorry for what I said. I'm a little on edge this morning, that's all."

"That's okay," Vanessa said with a smile. "I guess you're wondering why I invited you to lunch. I want to pick your brain."

Carrie's eyes widened. "About what? Don't tell me you want to become a P.I., too?"

"No, of course not. But I want Jim to stay here and to be happy."

"He seems happy to me," Carrie replied.

The waiter interrupted their conversation to deliver their meals. Carrie immediately began eating.

"I know, but he doesn't know anyone here except us, of course. I was thinking of having a party and inviting some eligible friends."

"Eligible?" Carrie asked, but the word stuck in her throat.

"Yeah. You know, single. I want Jim to find someone to settle down with, to be happy with."

"And you think he needs help?"

"Well, Carrie, he only knows family. We've got to expand his horizons a little. So tell me, what do you think about the women on this list?" She pulled a folded piece of paper from her purse.

Carrie started to refuse. Then she reached for the paper and unfolded it. "Stella? She's not single."

"Yes, she is. She and her boyfriend broke up."

"Well, there's no way I'd introduce her to *my* brother."

"Silly, of course not. You don't have a brother."

"Yes, but she's a Dolly Parton wannabe!"

"I think Dolly is a very nice person. She's always so sweet to everyone." Vanessa smiled.

"You can't say that about Stella!"

"Maybe not, but—but Stella has two large assets that men appreciate."

Carrie shoved the paper back to Vanessa. She picked up her fork and continued eating, only saying, "Your list is fine. I'm sure Jim will enjoy meeting so many eligible ladies."

"Well, when shall we have it?"

Carrie looked up, surprised. "Who is 'we', Tonto?"

"You and me, of course. I thought we'd play hostesses for the party. We can have it at my house and Betty will provide the food. We'll have to figure out what we can do to keep everyone having fun."

"Why don't you hire a band and roll up the rug in the family room? That should keep things hopping," Carrie suggested.

"Good idea! Now, let's see—"

"Vanessa, I was kidding. Poor Danny wouldn't get any sleep if you did that."

"Oops, I forgot about my baby brother. Okay, we'll just play CDs but we can dance. That would be fun."

"I—I don't think I'll be able to come."

"How can you say that? We haven't even picked a date yet."

"You know I'm not a party person, Vanessa. I never have been."

"But Jim will need all the support he can get."

"With all the women fawning over him? I don't think so."

"We're going to invite some men, too, of course. There wouldn't be much dancing going on with only Jim there. Shall I make a list of men we know?"

"No, I—I don't know any eligible men."

"Okay, I'll round up a few so we can dance, too."

Carrie ducked her head and ate quickly. As soon as she'd finished, she said, "I really need to get back to the office so Will and Jim can have lunch. They get hungry, you know." She stood, ready to leave.

"But we don't have our check yet," Vanessa pointed out. Then, as if she had a brilliant idea, she said, "I know. I haven't finished eating. Why don't you send Will and Jim here? I'll hold the table and they can call me on my cell phone and place their orders. Their food will be here when they arrive."

"Fine. Here's money for my lunch. I'll talk to you soon," Carrie said, and headed for the door.

Later when the switch had been completed, leaving

Carrie in the office on her own and the two men in the restaurant, Vanessa began again. "Oh, Jim, I'm thinking about having a party. Do you have any single male friends we can invite?"

Jim narrowed his eyes. "No. Why did you think I would?"

"Well, there are a lot of men in the marines. I thought maybe some of your friends were on leave here or might've come back to Dallas when they got out," Vanessa explained as she tasted the peach cobbler she'd ordered.

"You don't know any young men?" he asked, watching his sister.

"Yes, *I* do, but Carrie doesn't know many single men. I think she needs someone to make her feel…you know, pretty."

"She *is* pretty!" Jim returned, frowning at Vanessa.

"I know that, but I'm not sure she does."

Will spoke up. "Carrie does seem to have a limited social life…. Maybe I can come up with a few guys for you to invite."

"*I* think Carrie is just fine as she is," Jim said. "Has she asked you to set her up with someone?"

"No," Vanessa said calmly. "But I've known her for a long time. She has no one but us. I don't want her to feel…I don't know, like a fifth wheel. She needs her own personal family. You know?"

"I thought *we* were her family. That's what both of you told me," Jim pointed out.

"We are," Will said firmly. "But she might want to

have a family of her own sometime in the future. There's nothing wrong with that."

"I guess not," Jim agreed, but he didn't look happy about it.

Vanessa almost burst out laughing. She couldn't wait to get home to her mother and tell her about the results of their plan.

Chapter Nine

"I got my invitation to Vanessa's party."

Carrie nearly cringed at the sound of Jim's pronouncement several days later when they were working quietly at their computers. That party was looming like a big black hole at the end of her week.

After a moment she said, "Me, too."

"Are you going?" Jim asked casually.

That was the real issue. She dreaded going to this party, but she had to go. She couldn't bail on Vanessa.

"I have to," she said finally. "At least for a little while."

"Yeah, me, too."

She debated discussing it with Jim, then got a grip on herself and returned to the file she'd opened onscreen. She was on the verge of proving another insurance fraud and was eager to close the case. Something made her turn around, though. Some niggling sense of being watched. When she did, she found Jim standing beside her desk.

"Carrie, do you know how to dance?"

She stared up at him, her eyes wide. "Well, yes, sort of."

"What do you mean 'sort of'?"

"I used to dance some, but it's been a long time."

"Could you teach me to dance? I want to make Vanessa proud of me, but I've never been to a dance. It sounds so high school."

"Well, you can talk as well as dance."

"But that's what I'm telling you, Carrie. I don't know how to dance. I didn't go to dances in high school, and once I got into the military, it wasn't a necessary skill." When she didn't respond at once, he said, "Will said you would help me."

"I'm sure Vanessa can teach you. She knows all the latest steps."

"I don't want to ask Vanessa. I'd rather not confess my weaknesses to her."

Carrie knew she was losing the argument. But she knew teaching Jim to dance would involve touching. "Jim, I—" Oh, what was the sense? She knew she'd never win. "Okay. I can teach you enough to get by."

"I appreciate it, Carrie. I don't want to embarrass Vanessa."

"I don't think that's possible, Jim. Vanessa is very proud of you." Carrie turned back to her desk and began shuffling papers, trying to look busy. Jim didn't take the hint.

"Can we start tonight?" he asked. "The party's at the end of the week and I want to be prepared."

Carrie shrugged. "I guess so. For a little while."

"How about I take you out to dinner first?"

She swung around to stare at him. "No!" Then she lowered her voice and explained, "that's not necessary."

Jim raised one brow. "It seems fair to me. We'll stop somewhere on the way from work, get dinner and then practice dancing when we get home."

Carrie continued to stare at him, unable to think of a good reason to protest. She couldn't. She was stuck.

As if knowing he'd won this skirmish, Jim turned, picked up several files and said, "I'm going out for a couple of hours. See you when I get back."

Carrie stared at the door through which he'd disappeared. She couldn't believe she'd let him force her into another evening together.

No, that wasn't true. She'd *let* him, because she hadn't been prepared. If she had been, she would have managed to avoid being alone with him. So she needed to get her thoughts organized so she didn't lose ground tonight.

Maybe at the party she would find someone she was interested in. Someone besides Jim. She groaned. Life seemed to have gotten much more difficult since Jim came home. And she'd thought it a happy day when he'd walked into the office!

"Carrie, are you okay?" Will asked from his door.

"Oh, yes, of course, Will. I was just thinking about— about something."

"Something unpleasant?"

"Not exactly."

"Where's Jim?"

"He's out working on several cases."

Will propped himself against the door frame. "He's caught on pretty quickly, hasn't he?"

"Yes, he has."

She didn't look up until she realized Will was still standing there staring at her.

"Did you need something, Will?"

"No, honey, I was just thinking. So you think it will be all right for Jim to join us?"

"Has it been a week already?"

"Over a week, actually. I don't see any need to wait as long as you approve."

"Yes, Will, Jim is going to work out well, I'm sure." And that was true. She just wasn't sure that she could remain with them.

In spite of what Will said, Carrie knew the time might come when she'd have to leave her second home. That thought made her stomach queasy, but she was determined to face facts. Even so, she couldn't insist that Will send Jim away just because she had a crush on him.

"Okay, good. When he comes back in, I'll talk to him."

"Of course."

"If I don't hear him come in, you'll send him in to my office?"

"Yes, Will."

ON HIS WAY back to the office, Jim picked up his new cell phone and called the office.

"Greenfield and Associates." Carrie's crisp tones brought a smile to his lips.

"Hi, Carrie. Is Will in?"

"Yes, Jim. Just a minute."

Jim was glad when Carrie put him on hold for Will. He was anxious to tell him his news. "Will, I think I've got evidence on the Olney case. I'm coming back with the photos to check."

"Great! That's wonderful. And fast. Are you on your way back to the office now? I'd like to speak with you."

"Yeah, I'll see you in about five minutes." Jim paused, then asked, "Uh, Will, where is a nice restaurant to take a lady to dinner? It doesn't have to be fancy."

Jim could tell from the hesitation in Will's response that he was no doubt trying to guess the identity of the lady in question. For some reason, Jim didn't want to get into it—maybe because even he wasn't exactly sure why he was taking Carrie to dinner. He told himself it was payback for all her time, but he feared it went deeper than that.

First of all, he felt guilty. He hadn't exactly lied to Carrie when he said he couldn't dance. He'd managed to get around a dance floor before, though he suspected the women at Vanessa's party would expect more expertise than he had.

But why ask Carrie for help? asked a niggling voice inside his head.

Why, indeed. He could've asked Vanessa, after all, sure his youngest sister would have jumped at the chance to help. That he'd asked Carrie meant something he didn't want to admit.

No, he told himself. He didn't have to worry. He'd built up a wall of resistance to Carrie's charms, since he knew a relationship wasn't in his future. And Carrie wasn't even interested in him. In the end, then, Jim figured the dinner was harmless.

Thankfully Will didn't press him for details. He simply said, "There's a little Italian place called Amore over in Snider Plaza. Viv and I like it. It's cozy."

"Sounds good. Thanks." Then he said goodbye before Will's curiosity got the better of him.

When he got back to the office, he went directly in to see his boss.

"Everything okay?" Will asked as he directed him to a seat opposite his desk.

That question got Jim's attention. Did Carrie say something about him? Then he remembered he'd been with Greenfield and Associates over a week, and he realized the purpose of the talk. "The work? I like it. I know I still have a lot to learn, but you were right, it fits my skills."

Will sat back in his desk chair. "I think you can make a big difference in the amount of cases we process."

"Have you talked to Carrie about me joining you?" Jim wanted to be sure it was okay with her.

"Of course. And she agreed that you should."

"Then I'd like to be a part of your firm." Jim admitted then what he'd been thinking of for the past several days. "In fact, how much would it cost me to buy in as a partner?"

Will seemed surprised. "You have money to invest?"

He mentioned the amount he had available. "Is that sufficient to be a partner?"

"That'll buy you—" Will did some quick calculations "—thirty-five percent. Actually I'd love it. Now that we've got Danny, I'd been wanting to spend more time at home. Having you as a partner would take the load off. But you understand, Jim, that I'd have to consult

Carrie first. She bought twenty percent when her mother died. Even though I'd still hold the majority percentage, Carrie would be the deciding vote in any disagreement."

"Of course," Jim said. But he didn't share Will's confidence about Carrie's positive reaction. He couldn't read her facial expression when Will called her in and related the new development. She sat there blandly, with no hint of emotion in her demeanor. Finally she said, "Will, you know I would never vote against you."

"I don't think Will is suggesting we might come to blows over anything, Carrie," Jim said, smiling when she finally looked at him.

"Of course not," Will agreed, chuckling. Then he looked more serious. "But I do need to know if that's okay with you."

"Of course."

"Okay, we'll work things out as we go, as long as we're all in agreement." Will stood and shook Jim's hand.

Then Jim extended a hand to Carrie. She shook his hand, but pulled it away as soon as possible.

"If that's all, I'm in the middle of something," Carrie said, edging toward the door.

After she left the office, closing the door behind her, Will said, "Something seems to be bothering her."

"I don't think she's quite comfortable with me," Jim said. "But I'm working on it."

"Say, Vivian and I could take you and Carrie to dinner tonight to celebrate our agreement! That would—"

"Uh, Will, why don't we do that another night?"

"Sure." Will studied Jim. "Well, I'm glad we've settled the future at least."

Jim stood and shook Will's hand again. "I'm glad, too."

He returned to the outer office and settled behind his desk. After making notations in the two files he'd been working on, he turned on his computer and made the rounds of several sites he'd bookmarked.

When Carrie began packing up to go home, he said, "I thought we'd go to dinner on the way home. But if you prefer, I'll pick you up at quarter to six."

She appeared startled. "Really, Jim, there's no need—"

"I've already made the reservations. I'll see you in a little while." Then he bent his head as if he intended to end the debate.

After a moment of silence, when he refused to look up, Carrie left the office. Jim sat back and let out a deep breath. For a minute there he'd feared she would refuse once and for all.

He didn't want to examine why that thought was so disappointing.

OVER DINNER Jim kept the conversation on general subjects until Carrie lost that wide-eyed look. He teased her about her choice of meal, assuring her he could afford a more expensive dinner.

"But I like lasagna," Carrie protested. "And you ordered it, too."

"All right, I'll concede that point. Tell me how you and Vanessa became friends." He'd wondered about that all along.

"We met in college, at SMU."

"I know that, but— Well, people don't seem to

move outside their own group. Vanessa comes from money."

"Back then I did, too."

"What happened?"

"My father died suddenly. We—Mom and I—discovered we were sitting atop a house of cards that collapsed. He left a lot of debts." She said those words unemotionally, as if she'd said them all before.

"I'm sorry."

"You didn't exactly have it easy yourself," she pointed out. "Were your foster parents nice?"

"A couple of them were. One was...bad. They had sixteen children in their home, so they could collect more money. I was glad when they took me out of that home."

"Have you kept in touch with the other foster parents you had?"

"No. It wasn't like you see on television. It was a job for money. Or maybe it was me. I didn't trust any of them."

"Why the marines?"

"Because I was mad," Jim said with a soft laugh. "I wanted to hit someone. I got my shot, too, but I had a wise sergeant who taught me a lot."

"He taught you computer skills?"

"No, he taught me about being a man, about self-discipline, giving your word, things my dad might have taught me if he'd still been alive."

"It must've been hard," Carrie said softly.

"For both of us," he said. "It kind of sets us apart, doesn't it? I mean, I love Vanessa, but I'm not sure she will ever understand. And I hope she doesn't ever have to."

"Maybe not. But Rebecca and Rachel understand. And maybe David, when we find him."

"Do you think we will?"

"Of course. We found the rest of you, didn't we?"

"When are we going to start looking for David?"

"As soon as we get caught up on the insurance cases. We would've already been working on it, but Will signed with the third company and we got so far behind."

"I cleared up one of the cases today."

"Which one?" Carrie asked eagerly, her edginess disappearing completely.

Jim told her about the Olney case and the details of his discovery, pleased to see she accepted his work. Which meant whatever problem she had with him had nothing to do with his becoming a part of the firm.

So what was it?

He was convinced the problem was personal when they reached their apartments at the end of their meal. The closer they got to home, the more tense Carrie became.

"Sh—shall we practice in my apartment?" she asked.

"I think I've got less furniture, so why don't we use my place?"

"Do you have some CDs?"

"Yeah, a few."

"I'll go get some of mine and bring them over," she said, rushing away after he'd parked the car as if she was escaping.

He slowly got out of his car, keeping his gaze on Carrie as she rushed inside and up the stairs. If she showed that much eagerness running toward him, he'd be worried. Wouldn't he? After all, he had no intention of marrying and settling down.

That wouldn't be smart.

After he unlocked the door to his apartment, he did a visual sweep to be sure he hadn't left a mess. Not that he was a messy person. He'd been trained as a foster child to take care of what little he owned. The marines had completed his training.

Carrie's knock interrupted his thoughts. He opened the door to her.

"Come in," he said, stepping back and smiling.

She did so, but she didn't smile back. Nor did she look at him. Instead, she shuffled the CDs in her hands. "I thought these might work."

"I'm sure they will," he said, taking the CDs and looking at them. "Hey, you even brought some country-western. I like George Strait."

"Me, too. I didn't know whether you knew how to line dance."

"No, I don't. Do you?"

"A little. There are a few basic steps I can show you."

"Why don't we start with those?" he suggested.

"All right. If you'll stand behind me and do as I do, I think that will be easiest."

Jim put the music on and took his place behind Carrie. She was wearing wool pants that fit her snugly. It was a pleasure to watch her move—until he remembered he was supposed to be doing the same.

"Are you getting this basic step okay?" she asked over her shoulder.

"Uh, yeah. Maybe one more time."

She repeated the step. Then she moved back beside him. "Now we'll try it together." She slid her arm around his waist and instructed him to do the same to her.

Jim willingly did so, pulling her a little closer to him. Then he tried to untangle his feet to keep up with Carrie.

"Okay, good. Now you should spin me around under your arm," she instructed, and followed as he did so. "Now back to the original step."

They danced to the end of the song.

"You picked that up fast. What kind of dance do you want to do next?"

Jim shrugged his shoulders and picked up the CDs again. "How about a slow dance?" he asked, handing her a CD of romantic songs.

"Okay." She changed the CD, then she explained the steps.

When he held out his arms, however, she hesitated before she moved close to him. Close for her, anyway. Not close enough, for him.

After several moments he eased her slightly closer. A moment later she put more distance between them.

"Are we supposed to dance this far apart?" he asked.

"It's a good idea until you get to know your partner well."

"Don't we know each other well?"

She lowered her eyes. "Not really. And besides, you're practicing for Vanessa's party, not for dancing with me."

"Oh. So any of the women I dance with won't be surprised if I dance this far apart?" he persisted.

She glared at him now, a fire in her eyes he hadn't

seen most of the evening. "I'm sure they'll let you know if they are."

"What will they do?"

She dropped her arms from him and stepped back. "You're being difficult, Jim. I'm sure you've been around women who wanted to let you know that they were attracted to you. You're not a child!"

"No, I'm not. Have you ever let a man know you wanted him?"

"That's none of your business! I think it's time I go home now. I have some things to do before I go to bed. I'll see you at work tomorrow."

She rushed past him, but he caught her by the arm.

"I didn't mean to upset you, Carrie."

"Of course not. You couldn't upset me if you tried!" She raised her chin up, as if to punctuate her remark.

"Right."

She pulled away and again reached for the door.

"Don't forget your CDs," he called.

"Bring them with you to the office tomorrow!" And then she slammed his door behind her.

Chapter Ten

For the first time since she started working for Will, Carrie dreaded going to work the next morning. She was deliberately late, not wanting to run into Jim in the hallway or the parking lot. But at nine o'clock, she could delay no longer.

She opened the door to her apartment and peeked out. The way looked clear, so she stepped quietly into the hallway and locked her apartment door. Just as she started down the stairs, she heard a door open behind her.

Whirling around, she discovered Jim locking his door.

"Looks like we're both late this morning," he said without expression.

"Yes," she agreed, and turned and ran down the stairs.

"Hey, wait up." He hurried after her. "You want to share a ride this morning?"

She didn't look around. "No!"

He watched as she got in her car and drove away.

Jim stood there, staring after her. He'd waited until he heard her on the stairs before he'd come out, hoping a casual meeting would ease things at the office. Obviously he'd failed. He'd upset her last night.

"Damn," he said with a sigh. He'd really hoped they could become friends, share their problems, work as a team. Wasn't that what he'd been doing?

He thought back to his behavior last night. He'd pushed her because she was behaving like a nineteenth-century heroine. He'd been wrong to do that.

Getting in his new SUV, Jim had intended to follow Carrie to the office but she was already gone. When he got there, he noticed her car wasn't in the parking lot. He raced up the stairs to see if Will knew what was going on. That's when he found Vanessa seated at Carrie's desk.

"Good morning, Jim," she greeted him.

He gave her a hug before he asked, "Where's Carrie?"

"She called me early this morning to say she needed to be out of the office today to do some work and wanted me to hold down the fort."

"What about your classes?"

"Mostly I'm on independent studies. I can make my own schedule except for a couple of classes, so I fill in when Carrie needs a break," Vanessa assured him with a smile.

"Did she say what she'd be working on today?"

"No, she never tells me what she's working on."

"Look in that stack of files and see if you find one marked Riley," he suggested as he put his briefcase down on his desk.

Vanessa looked dubious about intruding into Carrie's files, but it was Jim asking.

Vanessa searched the cabinet. "I don't see a file marked Riley. Is that good?"

Jim frowned. "Not exactly."

"You mean Carrie is chasing after Riley today?" Will asked, coming out of his office.

"It's possible. His file is missing." Jim scanned Carrie's desk, looking for other files she might have kept separated, but he didn't see anything.

"I don't think Carrie would do that without checking with me first," Will said. "We usually discuss any new approach."

Jim didn't say anything, but he had his doubts about Carrie following that procedure today.

"By the way, did you make an appointment to see Michaels?" Will asked.

"Yeah, I'm having lunch with him today." Jim wasn't sure how good it was since he was sure he wouldn't be able to keep his mind on business with Carrie missing.

All morning at his desk, he worked on his new computer, updating files. Every time the door opened, which wasn't that often, he looked up, hoping to see Carrie stroll in.

No such luck.

A little before twelve, he gathered the files Michaels would be interested in and headed to the restaurant where they'd agreed to meet.

Much to his surprise, he found Carrie there. Before he could approach her to speak to her, she spotted him and gave a slight shake of her head that warned him to keep away. Could she be working a case?

He found Michaels and introduced himself, but his attention was divided between his conversation and Carrie and the group of women with whom she was eating.

When the women paid their bills and got up to leave,

he saw Carrie go into the ladies' room while the rest of them left. Fortunately, Michaels had to get back to the office. After shaking the man's hand, Jim went back in the restaurant and waited outside the restroom.

When Carrie opened the door to come out, he noticed her hair for the first time. It was done differently from the simple style she wore, more elaborate and stiff with spray. Carrie's hair was always soft, bouncy, inviting a man to run his hands through it....

Stop that! he told himself. He had no business thinking about Carrie in that way.

"Are you all right?" he asked her as she emerged from the ladies' room.

She jumped as if he'd shot her.

Drawing a deep breath, she said, "Yes, I am. Did the women all leave?"

"Yes, who were they?"

"Some beauticians and their customers. It was an impromptu gathering."

"I see you got your hair done. Will doesn't mind if you take off for personal things like that?"

Carrie stiffened. "Why don't you ask him?"

"I'm not the enemy, Carrie. I was just curious." Jim waited, hoping she would tell him what she was doing. Instead, she headed for the door to the parking lot.

He followed her, still hoping to make amends for whatever he'd done, whether it was last night or this morning. "Are you going back to the office now?"

"No, I'm going shopping." She got in her car and drove out of the parking lot.

When Jim got back to the office, he reported to Will,

on his lunch with Michaels, and about seeing Carrie. "I'm not trying to get her in trouble, Will, but it seems like she's behaving very strangely."

"You can't get her in trouble, Jim. She's a partner, remember? I'm sure she has a good reason for what she's doing."

"Yeah, but why is she so secretive about it?"

"I don't know." Will shook his head, then called, "Vanessa?" When she appeared at the door, he asked, "Where does Carrie usually go to get her hair done?"

Vanessa stared at Will. "You mean a beauty shop?"

He nodded.

"There's one on Park where she goes to get it cut, but that's only once every other month. Why?"

"Nothing, honey. Thanks."

Jim finally understood. "So she was undercover for some reason. I think it must be connected to the Riley case. But his wife doesn't work, does she?"

"I don't think so. Carrie has worked on that case mostly by herself."

"Okay. I'll try not to ask too many questions."

"Jim, in the years Carrie has been with me, I've never been cheated on her efforts, and I've come to trust her judgment. The only time I step in is when I think she's going to get in trouble."

Jim sighed. "I know. I just can't help worrying about her."

"She's taken self-defense courses, and she has a gun."

"Sometimes things happen so fast a gun can't help." He knew that all too well.

"Trust her, Jim. It's the only thing you can do. She

won't let me or you or anyone else take care of her." Will smiled at Jim, recognizing his frustration.

"Right."

Jim returned to his desk, checked a few things on his computer, then stood. "I'm going out for a little while, Vanessa. I have my cell phone with me if anything comes up."

Vanessa was reading a school text and looked up to smile and nod before returning to her studies.

He missed Carrie. She didn't always smile at him, but she always intrigued him. Then he reminded himself he had enough mysteries to solve in his files. He should concentrate on them instead of a certain blonde.

WHEN CARRIE GOT to her complex that evening, later than she'd expected, she was exhausted. Undercover work was often necessary, seldom fun and always tiring. She didn't like lying to people.

She slowly climbed the stairs to her apartment, thinking only of changing clothes and eating the pizza she'd ordered for delivery. She was even too tired to pick it up on the way home.

As she was unlocking her door, Jim's door opened behind her and he asked, "Carrie, are you all right?"

She didn't turn around. "Of course I am. I'm a little tired, that's all."

"A long day at the office?" he taunted.

"Yes, as a matter of fact, it was." She opened the door but before she could close it, Jim followed her in. "Go away!"

"I just wanted to return your CDs and make sure

you're okay." He put them on the table. "Do you have food here for dinner?" He opened her refrigerator and then her pantry. "Don't you shop?"

He'd pushed her to the limit. "Get out of my apartment! I can take care of myself!"

In a soothing voice that agitated her even more, he said, "I'm sure you can. How about something—Chinese, a pi—"

"I already ordered a pizza. Are you satisfied?" she said sarcastically as she flung herself down on the sofa. At least she'd get rid of him, now that he knew her nutritional needs were being met.

It didn't. Instead, he joined her on the couch.

"I've been pacing the floor worrying about you," he said.

"Worrying about me? Afraid I'm not giving my all to the partnership?" she asked bitterly.

"No, because I figured out that you were out on the Riley case." Before she could protest, he continued, "I'm hoping when you explain it, I'll learn more about the work I'll be doing one day."

So he trusted her? That was a pleasing thought, one that loosened her tongue. "I found out Riley's brother, Charles, is married to a beautician. So I made an appointment to get my hair done. I chatted with Susie, we hit it off, and a bunch of us went to lunch."

"What did you learn?"

"Not a lot. Except she doesn't like her husband to hang out with his brother, because she considers him to be a liar and a cheat. But Charles has always looked up to his big brother."

"Interesting."

"Susie keeps him on a short leash. She said she learned early in their marriage not to let him carry the checkbook because he'd give his brother whatever he asked for."

"So that's why your hair is like that," he blurted, as if he'd finally realized why. "I don't think it's an improvement."

"Susie said it was a vast improvement over my old style," she assured him with a grin. "It's been driving me crazy ever since. I want to stick my head under a sink and wash all that hairspray out."

Jim reached up and touched it. "It's like a piece of cardboard."

"I know," Carrie agreed, trying to run her fingers through it, but finding it impossible to do. With a sigh, she said, "After that, I went shopping where Riley's sister works. Susie told me to go, so I introduced myself as a client of hers. I finally bought something to wear to Vanessa's party because I had to buy something after spending three hours there trying on clothes."

"Can't you charge it to the firm?" Jim asked.

"No. It's bad enough that I was shopping. I don't think I can ask Will—or you—to pay for it."

"Did you find out anything?"

"Yes. Riley and his wife are going to Vegas, right after they get the settlement check. His wife had come shopping there to buy a wardrobe for the trip."

Jim sat up straight. "That's big, Carrie. Did you find out when they're going or where they'll be staying?"

"Of course," she said smugly before bursting out laughing at Jim's expression.

"I think that's where you have it over me and Will. I can't see men shopping and getting that kind of information!"

"Men gossip as much as women do," she told him, raising one eyebrow as if daring him to disagree.

"Yeah, but it's usually about a football team or some other sports-related topic."

A knock on the door interrupted their conversation and Jim stood and took out his billfold.

"I have the money for the pizza," Carrie said, reaching for her purse.

"Nope. This one's on me." He paid for the pizza and took it from the teenager standing at the door, giving him a good tip.

"Isn't Carrie here?" the boy asked, trying to look over Jim's shoulders.

"I'm here, Max. Thanks," Carrie said, moving to the door.

"Sure thing, Carrie. Enjoy." Then he backed away from the door before turning and running down the stairs.

"I didn't know you ordered from the pizza place all the time," Jim said, raising an eyebrow.

"Not that often, but Max always delivers for me."

"Yeah, I got that. He seemed more interested in you than the tip."

"That's not true. Do you want Diet Coke, milk or water with your pizza? I'm afraid that's all the choices I have tonight."

"I'll take Diet Coke," he said, moving to the coffee table with the pizza box.

She brought him his drink as well as her own and they settled down for their impromptu dinner.

"Will's going to be really impressed with your news, Carrie," Jim said.

"Maybe. It means he'll need to send me to Vegas to take pictures. That will be costly."

Jim stopped the pizza halfway to his mouth. "Wait a minute. You don't think you're going alone to Vegas to take pictures, do you?"

"Of course I am. What would be the point of two of us going?" She took a bite of pizza and closed her eyes to enjoy the taste. When she opened them, Jim had put his pizza back on his plate and was staring at her.

"Carrie, that wouldn't be safe and you know it! Will has said this man is dangerous. If he saw you taking pictures, he'd kill you before he'd let you get away."

"Jim, I'm not an amateur. I've taken pictures without people ever realizing it. I'll be perfectly fine."

"We'll talk to Will about it. I don't think he'll approve."

"So what? You're going to volunteer to go with me? That won't work."

"Why not?"

"Because we'd be in separate rooms. I might forget to let you know I was going out. Or Riley might follow me back to my room and you'd never know it."

Jim stared at her, opening his mouth to protest, then closing it. He only said, "We'll discuss it with Will."

"I intended to do that all along." Her chin was in the air and he knew he'd seriously offended her.

"Fine, we'll discuss it as partners tomorrow. You will be there tomorrow, won't you?"

"Of course."

He rose, taking one more piece of pizza with him. "Then I'll go home and get some rest. Thanks for sharing your pizza."

"Thanks for *buying* my pizza. Sure you don't want more of it?"

"Nope. I've got enough. Good work today," he added, but she didn't respond to his praise.

Jim hurried into his apartment and grabbed the phone, putting the pizza on the counter and forgetting it. He dialed Will's number at home.

"Is Will there?" he asked Betty. "It's Jim."

"He's having dinner, Jim. Can he call you later?"

"Yes, of course. That will be fine." It wasn't fair to interrupt a man's dinner. But he had to talk to him before Carrie did. He had to make sure she didn't go to Vegas alone.

A FEW MINUTES AFTER Jim left her apartment, after she'd finished her pizza, Carrie decided to call Will. She wanted to tell him her good news, but she also wanted to talk to him before Jim started in.

She was not going to be protected!

When Betty asked if Will could call her back after dinner, she agreed, not seeing any need to rush. She was going to be home all evening. But it was important to talk to Will before Jim did.

WHEN WILL AND VIVIAN LEFT the dining room, they intended to go upstairs and play a little while with Danny. They did so each evening before they put him to bed.

Before they could escape, Betty delivered the two messages she had for Will.

"Did either of them say what the call was about?" Will asked, frowning.

"No, sir. Jim sounded more urgent, but Carrie sounded normal."

"All right, Betty. Thanks."

"Do you want to call them before you come up?" Vivian asked.

"No, I'll call after we get Danny to bed. They're probably upset with each other. I think I might as well get used to their arguing. They seem to strike sparks off each other."

Vivian smiled.

Chapter Eleven

Carrie prepared for work the next morning, worried about her conversation with Will last night. He'd talked to Jim already and congratulated her on her discoveries. He had said they'd have a meeting this morning to determine their next step.

She'd wanted to question the necessity of bringing in Jim, but before she could do so, Will reminded her that though the paperwork would take awhile essentially he was a partner in the firm also, and he got to vote on everything.

When she reached the office, both men were already there, in Will's office.

"Carrie? Is that you?" Will called out.

"Yes, it's me," she said, going to his office door.

"Want to join us? I brought doughnuts."

No, she didn't want to join them, but if she didn't, she'd have to explain why. She got a Diet Coke out of the small refrigerator. Then she entered Will's office and took the second wing chair beside Jim's.

"Good morning." Carrie looked at Will, not Jim.

"I'll take one, Will. I didn't have much breakfast this morning."

She could feel Jim's gaze on her as she reached for a doughnut, but she ignored him.

After they ate and she repeated her information on the Riley case, Will asked, "Did you get the date of their trip?"

"They're leaving the end of next week. I called the hotel in Vegas last night and confirmed their reservation."

"Jim says you're thinking about going on the trip alone," Will said calmly.

"I don't see a need for the expense for two of us to go. Unless we were sharing a room, I'd still be alone."

"That's why Jim suggested the two of you go, posing as a married couple," Will said.

Carrie choked on her drink. "What?"

Jim defended his suggestion. "You're the one who pointed out that unless we were sharing a room, you wouldn't be protected. It's the safest way."

Though she glared at Jim, Carrie turned to Will to present her argument. "It probably won't even be necessary for me to check into the hotel. I can just hang around for a couple of hours and probably get all the proof I need."

"There's no guarantee that he'll expose himself that quickly," Jim said. "And if he doesn't, then the price of your ticket will have been wasted."

"So, if it's wasted, I won't bill the firm. I'll pay for it myself!" she snapped.

"Carrie, you know we're not concerned with the cost. We're concerned with your safety." Will smiled gently at her, and Carrie ground her teeth.

"I know, Will, but this is my case. I can handle it."

"I've told you from the beginning that I didn't like this case, Carrie. And we've always worked together when the case demands it. I think Jim's idea is a good one. He helps you with this case and you can help him with some of his. It's always been the way we worked."

Carrie let out a big sigh. "I know. Look, I apologize. I just don't adjust to change easily. But I understand. Jim can go to Vegas and get the proof. That will be fine."

Both men stared at her. Then Jim spoke. "No, Carrie, I wasn't trying to take your case from you. That wasn't it at all. I still think the best way is for both of us to go."

Carrie stared straight ahead and said nothing.

Like Solomon, Will stepped in. "We've got some time to decide how to handle it. Let's wait a couple of days. Maybe we'll take it up next Monday."

When no one protested his decision, Will smiled. "So both of you will be coming to the party tomorrow night, right?"

They both nodded without enthusiasm.

"Vanessa is so excited," Will said. "I'm not sure why, but I think she may have invited someone she's interested in, but she doesn't want us to know. Got any ideas about that, Carrie?"

Carrie frowned. "No, I don't think so. She said she was going to invite some guys, but she didn't specify anyone in particular."

"I think," Jim began, his gaze shifting from Carrie to Will and back again, "she's trying to do a little matchmaking. That would account for the excitement she's feeling. It's a game women like to play."

Carrie stared at him. "And you don't mind?" she asked carefully.

"It's none of my business," he said with a shrug.

"It's not? But you're the one she's wanting to match up with someone," Carrie pointed out.

"Not me. It's *you* she's planning the future for," Jim said.

"Uh, maybe there's a misunderstanding," Will suggested. "I thought she just wanted to expand your circle of acquaintances. She knows you work too hard, Carrie. And, Jim, you just got to town. I think she's wanting you to find some friends other than family."

Neither Jim nor Carrie responded to Will's suggestion and they changed the subject back to business. After a few more minutes, the two of them went back to their desks.

Carrie went through her files and updated them from her day yesterday. Her concentration was broken by Jim's question. "Do you believe Will's take on tomorrow night?"

Carrie sent him a cautious look. "Maybe."

"Vanessa told you she was trying to set me up?"

"I'm not sure I should—"

"Because that's what she told me, only she was talking about *you*," Jim said firmly. "I'm not mistaken about that."

"She told me the purpose of the party was to set *you* up. I'm not mistaken about *that!*" She looked back down at her files, not wanting to face Jim.

"We could mess up her plans by not going to the party," he suggested.

That remark brought her head back up. "We can't do

that to Vanessa. Even if she is hoping to match either of us up, it's not a crime. She would be devastated if we didn't show."

Jim stood and crossed over to her desk, hitching his hip onto a corner. "You're a very loyal friend, Carrie."

She just shrugged and continued to work, but Jim didn't go away, as she'd hoped.

"Let's make a deal," he said softly.

"What are you talking about?"

"Let's agree that if either of us needs rescuing, the other will come to his or her aid."

"How would we know?"

Jim paused, then said, "How about if I wink at you, or you wink at me?"

"I doubt that you'll need that signal," Carrie said in exasperation. She didn't want to betray Vanessa. If she wanted her brother to find his true love at her party, Carrie didn't feel she should intervene.

"Just in case I—or you—do, how about a wink?"

"I suppose," Carrie said slowly. "But only if it's really necessary."

"Right. What kind of dress did you buy for the party?"

Why did he care? she thought. And why did she tell him, "A light blue party dress."

"Sounds like the perfect color for you."

"Thank you. What are you wearing?" What was wrong with her? She didn't even want to go to the party, let alone care about Jim's clothing.

"Vanessa said I should wear a suit, so I'll wear the only one I own. Navy blue."

"I'm glad you had one. I mean you must not've had a big need for one while you were in the marines."

"No, but I was part of a wedding party for one of my buddies. I bought the suit for that occasion."

The phone rang, putting an end to their conversation, which had become too involved. Carrie didn't want to know too much about Jim, about his wardrobe or his past. She was already too attracted to him.

"Jim, it's Mr. Michaels calling for you."

When Jim took the call, Carrie tried to organize her day. She would prefer to work outside the office today, but there was no call to do so.

Jim hung up the phone quickly and asked, "Carrie, what do you have planned for today?"

"Just regular stuff. Why?"

"I need some help on a case for Michaels. They're almost ready to pay on a claim here in town, but something happened to make them question their decision. I think it's a case where some undercover work would help. The wife has been talking to friends, telling them they're about to come into some money. Could you make contact with her?"

Carrie agreed to work the case and Jim gave her some leads. Since the wife was a schoolteacher in a local elementary school, Carrie suggested, "I could pretend to be registering my child in school, asking to meet the teacher."

"How about we go as a married couple, checking out the school for a possible move?" Jim said. "Maybe a friend recommended her as the preferred teacher."

"I suppose we could do that. I'd need to go home to change." Her jeans wouldn't do.

"Okay, I'll pick you up in half an hour."

"Let me check with Will first." She stepped into Will's office and filled him in.

"No problem," Will said. "I'll be in the office all day, so I can handle the phone."

After clearing her desk, Carrie hurried downstairs to her car and drove home. She dressed in a tailored pant suit and short-sleeved cranberry sweater. Casual chic, she decided with a nod. She just finished combing her hair when Jim knocked on her door. She swung it open. "I'm ready."

Jim's eyes swept her from head to toe. What was with this man that just his gaze set her skin to tingling? She had the distinct feeling that he saw right through her clothes.

"You certainly are," he said. "Except for one thing. We have to pick up a wedding band for you. Will told me about a jeweler near the office."

A wedding band. How many times had Carrie imagined Jim would say those words to her? In her fantasies, they'd spent hours shopping the Dallas stores, hand in hand, looking for just the perfect ring. It had always been a platinum band studded with diamonds. And when he put it on her finger, Jim had looked her deep in her eyes and pledged his undying love. Their engagement was always sealed with a kiss that curled her toes.

There'd be none of that now. No hand-holding, no vows and certainly no kisses. Just a sham.

But, she reminded herself, that was for the best. What she had with Jim was strictly professional. At times, even that was too much.

"What about you?" she asked. "Don't you need a ring, too?"

"We'll see."

Carrie left the conversation there, not intending to force the issue, but when they got to the jewelry store, Jim asked about matching bands. Fifteen minutes later, they had beautiful gold bands.

"We'll need these for the trip to Vegas, too," Jim said, "so don't lose yours."

"I wasn't planning on losing it," Carrie said. "But I don't think we've come to a conclusion on the Vegas trip."

Jim just smiled.

AT THE END of their successful day, in which they'd gotten exactly what they needed, Jim asked Carrie if she wanted to have dinner before they went back home.

"No, thank you. I'm a little tired."

"I can see why. Telling lies all day and being careful not to get our wires crossed is difficult."

"You'll get used to it," Carrie said with a sigh.

"I could order us another pizza so you wouldn't have to cook for yourself," he suggested.

"I'll just have a salad. Too much pizza isn't good for me."

"You can't be worrying about your figure, Carrie. You look perfect to me."

He was doing it again. And again Carrie could feel her cheeks heating up. "Thanks, but I have to be careful."

As they stopped outside their apartments, he said, "Want to ride with me to Vanessa's party tomorrow evening?"

"I can't. I'm one of the hostesses, so I promised her I'd come straight over from work." She nervously pushed her hair behind her left ear, to keep it out of her face.

"That's how you know she's matchmaking?"

"For you, not me."

"Don't be too sure of that, Carrie. And don't forget our sign when either of us needs rescuing."

"I haven't forgotten."

She slipped into her apartment and closed the door behind her, grateful for the solitude. But when she reached into the fridge for the salad fixings, the light sparkled off her gold wedding band, and once again thoughts intruded on her peace.

The ring had to go. It winked at her like a neon sign. "It's all a ruse," it blinked. "You'll never get married for real. You'll always be alone."

Carrie took it off and put it back in the box, which she put on top of the fridge.

As she fixed her dinner, she couldn't help looking down at her now-bare, lonely finger.

FRIDAY'S WORKDAY seemed long to Carrie. She'd told Will and Jim she'd be leaving about four that afternoon to go to Vanessa's home to get ready for the party.

Will came out of his office at 3:45 and told her to go. "I don't think you're getting anything done anyway. Am I right, Jim?"

"Could be," Jim said with a grin. "I didn't notice, of course, but her pacing around the office has been a little distracting."

"Thanks a lot, Jim." Carrie looked at Will. "Okay, I'll

go and quit disturbing Jim. I wouldn't want him to lose work time because of me."

"Good," Will agreed. "I'll see you in a couple of hours. We'll be there, but we're going to stay upstairs unless things get out of hand. But I figure we can rely on Jim to keep everything in order."

"Hey, I'll do my best."

Carrie headed for the door. "I'm sure he'll do fine. Vanessa doesn't have friends who don't know how to behave."

Once she reached Vanessa's, she hurried into the house, taking her clothes to change into for the party.

Vanessa came running down the stairs to greet her. "Carrie, I'm so excited. We should have parties more often. They're so exhilarating."

"Did Stella say she was coming?"

"She never turns down a party."

"I don't think she's right for Jim. I hope you invited other girls for him." Carrie didn't look at Vanessa as she spoke.

"Of course. Just because he's my brother doesn't mean I get to make all his choices for him," Vanessa explained.

"No, I suppose not."

"Come on upstairs." Vanessa led the way up the stairs to her room. After admiring Carrie's dress, Vanessa pulled out the list of things that needed to be done. They divided up the chores and Carrie headed to the kitchen to see if Betty needed help.

Vanessa picked out the CDs for the party and arranged them in order. Then she placed the flower arrangements in their proper spots before she found the serving pieces for the dishes that would be on the buffet.

"How's it going in here?" she said as she stuck her head in the kitchen.

Betty was the one who replied. "Carrie has a dab hand in the kitchen."

"That's high praise from you, Betty. But I just did what you told me to do." Then Carrie turned to Vanessa. "How's your work coming?"

"I'm done. I'm ready to go take my shower and get dressed."

"I can finish up, Carrie, if you need to go, too," Betty assured her.

"That's okay. I want to cut up my fudge and arrange it on this plate."

"Well, I won't object," Betty said. "That will give me time to ice the carrot cake."

"Oh, I love carrot cake."

"Just do me a favor. When it's time to eat dessert, cut the first piece. Otherwise, no one will dare cut it and my carrot cake will go to waste."

"I promise I'll do that for you…with pleasure!" Carrie agreed with a grin.

THE PARTY WAS to begin at seven, so at six-thirty, Carrie and Vanessa, their preparations complete, descended to the first floor to do a final check.

Betty had the buffet set up in the den, and the rug removed, the furniture having been pushed back along the walls. In the dining room, Betty had set up the desserts for later in the evening. The table was full.

"How many people did you say are coming?" Carrie asked.

"Well, I invited thirty-five people and I got forty-one acceptances."

Carrie shook her head. "You're the only person I know who could receive more acceptances than she sent out invitations."

"Well, I agreed when people asked if they could bring a friend. According to my calculations, we'll have more males than females. And I don't want you avoiding everyone like you usually do. I want you to join in the fun."

"I'll try," Carrie promised with a sinking heart. She really didn't enjoy parties, but she'd make an effort tonight. Especially since she would be looking for a guy to use as an excuse to avoid some of Vanessa's invitations.

"Did Jim say when he'd get here?" Vanessa asked.

"No, he didn't."

"So you two didn't discuss the party at all?"

Carrie couldn't meet Vanessa's gaze. She straightened one of the dessert forks as she said, "We mentioned it once or twice, but mostly we discuss business at work."

"How dull!"

"Actually, we think it's interesting. And Jim is doing a good job. He's impressed one of our clients and solved a couple cases since he started."

"Good. I want him to do well. And you think he likes it?"

"Yes, I'm sure he does."

"That's—"

Vanessa stopped because the doorbell sounded. She linked her arm with Carrie's. "Our first guest has arrived. Let's get the party started."

Chapter Twelve

By seven-thirty, the music was playing, people were dancing both in the den and out on the patio, and everyone expected had arrived.

Carrie danced with several men, but she kept her gaze focused on Jim as he danced by her, his arm around a statuesque redhead. They were well matched, Carrie decided with a sigh, and vowed to give her full attention to the man she was dancing with.

Someone caught her hand and she looked up to find the dance had ended and Jim was holding it. "Hi, how are you doing?"

"You tell me, teacher," he said, pulling her into his arms. The music had started again and he moved them out into the center of the floor. "Who were you dancing with?" he whispered.

She looked up, startled. "Um, someone named Mike, a lawyer."

"You don't know his last name?"

"No. Is it important?"

"Nope. How am I doing, by the way?"

"If you're talking about your dancing, I think you were faking it when you said you needed lessons," she said, looking up at him with a challenge in her gaze.

He laughed and spun her around. "I knew how to dance, but I was a little rusty. You helped me get warmed up."

"I'm so glad I could be of service," she returned, a touch of sarcasm in her voice.

"I have a question for you. I should have asked it before. What do you tell people when they ask what you do for a living?"

Carrie quickly looked up and then away. "I lie. People get weird if I say I'm a P.I., so I tell them I'm a receptionist. Even Vanessa didn't know for a long time."

"Hmm, what's a good answer for me? I don't think receptionist will do."

"No, but you could say you work for an insurance company and still be telling the truth."

"Man, I should've thought of that."

"What did you tell Miranda?"

"Is that the redhead's name? I told her I wasn't sure what I was going to do yet. After all, I've only been back in the States a couple of weeks."

"That's not a bad answer."

"Thanks," Jim said with a laugh and another spin.

As they danced, Carrie felt herself move closer to Jim involuntarily, and she apologized as she tried to pull away from him.

"I told you people dance closer together, Carrie," he whispered in her ear. "Miranda certainly did, so I think it's all right."

That may be true, Carrie thought, but it wouldn't be

happening with them. Too close was too dangerous. She could feel his arms around her like bands of steel, and his chest was rock hard, no doubt courtesy of his military days. Even his thighs were muscular as they pressed against hers, sending her on a sensory sojourn that could only lead to trouble.

She backed away, putting a good foot between them, and finished the dance. Despite the distance, she enjoyed dancing with Jim and was disappointed when the music ended. She smiled at Jim and turned toward the edge of the room.

"Want to go again?"

"Don't be silly. Vanessa would be very disappointed if I kept you from the other ladies. You know that." She smiled and turned away again.

He let her go, of course. Several women were approaching him. The Dallas ladies weren't shy about introducing themselves to a man they wanted to dance with. Except for her. She'd never been good about that.

Vanessa met her as she came off the dance floor. "Is Jim having a good time?"

She looked over her shoulder at Jim. "It looks like it to me." Since he was surrounded by several women, she figured he wouldn't be doing any complaining. Or winking of his eye.

An hour later, Carrie was tired of dancing. She sat out several dances, visiting with old friends. Vanessa, she noticed, had been dancing with a different guy every song, but for the last two, she stayed with the same partner. He was tall, handsome, but Carrie didn't know his name. She asked a friend and discovered his first name was Trevor.

Jim danced by then, with Stella pressed up against him. Carrie was smiling ruefully until Jim looked directly at her and winked.

Surely she'd imagined it.

Jim swung his partner around and came back past Carrie and winked again. This time it was unmistakable.

She drew a deep breath and stood up to tap Stella on the shoulder, but before she could do so, the song ended. She stepped closer to Jim. "May I have the next dance, Jim?"

"I'd love to. Thanks, Stella."

"Wait a minute. I'm not through with him!" Stella protested, batting her eyelashes at Jim.

"Sorry. Maybe you can catch him again later," Carrie said, easily moving into Jim's embrace as a new song began.

He pulled her close against him and danced immediately to the French doors that led out to the patio. Once they were safely down the flagstone steps, they continued to dance in the dim light.

"Good job, honey. I don't think I could take another dance with dear Stella," Jim whispered.

"I don't like her, either, but Vanessa thought you should have different choices."

"I notice she's not making a lot of choices for herself. Who is the guy she's dancing with?"

"One of my friends said his name is Trevor, but I don't know him. He's very handsome."

"Yeah, but Trevor? We didn't get many of those kind in the marines."

"What kind?"

"People named Trevor or Windsor. You know, trust-fund babies."

"No, I guess you wouldn't," Carrie agreed with a smile. "But I don't know for sure that he has a trust fund."

"Hopefully Vanessa will change partners now. Three dances in a row with the same guy shows a little too much partiality."

"Wow. You're strict on your baby sister, aren't you?" Carrie was pretty sure Vanessa wouldn't appreciate Jim's ideas on how she should run her life. Vivian trusted Vanessa to make her own decisions.

"I tell you what. Since it's time for dessert, you grab a table for four and invite Vanessa to join us. I'll go get us some desserts. Do you have any preferences?"

"Anything chocolate. And a piece of the carrot cake. I promised Betty."

When the music ended, Vanessa invited everyone to enjoy dessert. As the guests surged to the dining room, Carrie waved Vanessa over and invited her to join her. "I'll save the table while you find someone to ask."

"Okay, I'll be right back."

True to her word, Vanessa was back in no time.

"Whom did you invite?" Carrie asked.

"Trevor Williams. Did you meet him?"

"No, I don't think I did. Is he new to the area?"

"No, I've known him for a while, but not well. He came with Graham Wilson tonight. We're getting along very well," Vanessa said with a self-satisfied smile.

"So I noticed. Jim did, too."

"Oh, was it obvious?"

"Well, yes. You danced three straight dances with him." She smiled as Vanessa's cheeks turned red.

"I didn't realize it was that many. We just kept talking and the music would start up again...I'll try not to dance with him again."

"You make it sound like that might be hard," Carrie teased.

Before Vanessa could protest, Jim reached their table. He managed three plates, one with fudge and two with carrot cake. "I couldn't handle another plate, so we'll have to share the fudge." He set the dishes down and then took a seat. "Hi, Vanessa. Great party. Who's joining us?"

Trevor reached their table just as Vanessa answered. She made the introductions and they all settled in for a sugar fix. After he'd finished his piece of carrot cake, Jim asked Trevor what he did for a living.

"I'm in real estate," Trevor said. "You need a house?"

Jim smiled but shook his head. "Not yet. I just got out of the service."

"You mean the army?"

"No, the marines."

"Did you have to go overseas?"

"Yes, I did."

"I'm against sending troops overseas. I think America should stay uninvolved in other countries' problems. We need to downsize our troops, not increase them."

Jim took a bite of fudge. "This is good, Carrie. Did you make it?"

"Yes, I did," she said, recognizing that Jim was trying to change the subject.

Trevor, however, seemed to be intent upon making sure Jim understood him. "I mean, I'm sure you worked hard, but it seems to me we shouldn't be killing other people. Did you have to kill someone?"

Jim looked at Trevor. "Yes, I did."

"Well, I think that's despicable," Trevor announced, withdrawing just the slightest amount from Jim.

"Jim is my brother," Vanessa said clearly. She hadn't indicated their relationship earlier. "And Wally, my second brother, was killed overseas."

"And that's my point exactly. We shouldn't be trying to kill people. You should've found a nice job after college and not gone into the marines."

"Is that what you did? Found a nice job after college?" Jim asked casually.

"Well, I started to work about a year later. I did some traveling first."

"Trust fund?" Jim asked.

"Yeah, my old man made a bunch of cash shipping ammo overseas."

"Good thing he has nothing against war, isn't it? Otherwise, you might not have gotten to travel." Jim turned to Carrie and offered her a second piece of fudge.

"No, thanks, Jim. You go ahead and eat it."

Trevor, in the meantime, was protesting, "My father didn't furnish ammo to the enemy, I can assure you."

"Really? So he only shipped to U.S. depots?"

"Well, no, but— I'm sure he only shipped to proper companies."

"Wait a minute. Do you mean he shipped to people other than the U.S.?" Vanessa questioned.

"Probably not," Trevor hurriedly said.

"But you don't really know, do you?"

"Easy, Vanessa," Jim said softly. "He could be telling the truth."

"No! He doesn't even know. He's just guessing!"

"Come on, Vanessa," Trevor began. "I doubt that my father would make money at our fighting troops' expense."

"It makes life easy for you when you don't know, doesn't it?" Vanessa said, glaring at him. She jumped up from the table and walked away.

"See what you did?" Trevor demanded, glaring at Jim.

Jim nodded, but didn't look very concerned.

Once Trevor had stalked away, Carrie asked, "How did you know?"

"I didn't. But who would name his kid Trevor?"

"Jim, you're being absurd. There's nothing wrong with that name."

"Would you name your kid Trevor?"

"No," she assured him, "but that doesn't make it a bad name."

"Whatever you say. How about another dance?"

"We can't," she teased. "We've already danced together twice, and you said three times was too often."

"Damn! Hoist on my own petard."

Carrie laughed. "Careful, you'll ruin your tough-guy image."

"Ah, right. I can't use words like *petard* in front of other people. All right, I'll take our dishes back and—"

He was interrupted by a young lady soliciting his hand for a dance.

"You go ahead, and I'll return our dishes," Carrie

said. Actually, she looked forward to checking with Betty and Peter in the kitchen.

When she reached the kitchen, she found Will there, too. "Is there a problem?"

"No. I'm downstairs to fix a tray for Vivian and me. How's the party going?"

"It's fine. It's a beautiful night for it."

"Meet anyone interesting?"

She gave Will a droll look. "No, I haven't. I thought Vanessa had, but I think Jim put a spoke in his wheel."

"Jim's a good man," Peter said solemnly.

"Yes, he is, Peter," Will agreed. "Now, Carrie, get back out there and find a nice guy for you."

"Right," she agreed, but she resisted Will's urging. She wasn't in the mood to find a nice guy. Not tonight.

She wandered back into the den, where in her role as cohostess, she invited a man to dance. Then she introduced him to a friend.

With a sigh, Carrie looked across the dance floor only to encounter Jim, dancing again with Stella. There was no doubting his wink.

Debating her options, she hesitated, but Jim swung his partner around and winked again, looking absolutely miserable. Carrie stepped onto the dance floor and made her way to the couple. She tapped Stella on the shoulder. "Mind if I cut in?"

Stella glared at Carrie. "You've already cut in once."

"Actually, I didn't. The music ended."

"Well, I don't want to give up my partner." Stella moved closer to Jim.

"Uh, Stella," Jim began, "maybe we can dance together later. But I think—" As if on cue, the music ended. "There you go. Now I'll dance the next one with Carrie."

"And maybe I'll interrupt her dance," Stella said, glaring at Carrie.

Fortunately for Jim, one of Carrie's earlier partners asked Stella to dance.

"And hopefully he'll keep her busy for a while," Jim murmured.

"Are you allergic to her?" Carrie asked. "Every time you've danced with her, you've winked at me."

"Yep, that's right. I'm allergic to women who *think* they're sexy. And I've been waiting for you to wink at me, but you seem perfectly happy with the men you've met. You even asked that last one to dance."

"I asked you to dance, too, remember?"

"Yeah, but only because I winked at you," he pointed out as he danced them out to the patio again.

This time, dancing with Jim felt good. She loved the feel of his hand on her back, how his other hand lightly held hers. Their bodies moved as one, swaying with the beat. Despite what he'd said, Jim was a good dancer.

"Mmm, I like it out here," she said after a deep breath. "Vivian's garden smells delightful. And it's so beautiful."

"Does she do all this by herself, or just direct Peter?"

"She does most of it herself. Of course, when she got too big during her pregnancy, she had to hand over the tools to Peter. But she's gotten back out since Danny was born. Of course, she might not have the time for it if she didn't have Betty. She's such a treasure."

Jim steered her into the shadows of a tree lit only by dim landscaping lights. They had left the noise of the party behind them, now only a distant hum that lulled her. If she allowed herself, Carrie knew she'd admit this was one of the most romantic encounters of her life. Good music to dance to, a handsome man to hold her, a moonlit night to hide in... This was just as it was in her fantasies. Maybe even better, since this Jim was flesh and blood.

She rested her head on his shoulder and let herself fall under his spell. His nearness worked magic on her, and in a flash the stoic marine was transformed into a hot-blooded man. A man who set her own blood to the flash point.

She couldn't hear the music anymore, but it didn't matter. They continued to move to the beat inside their heads, their bodies now pressed tightly against each other, breast to chest, thigh to thigh. It was heaven, and she never wanted it to end.

But then Jim pulled back, and Carrie thought her world had come crashing down—until he lowered his head and captured her lips in a searing kiss.

Chapter Thirteen

Jim couldn't believe how good Carrie felt in his arms. She was the softest thing he'd touched in years. Her lips were like pillows, and she tasted of chocolate. Why'd it take him so long to kiss her, when he'd been aching to do it since he'd first walked through their office doorway?

He deepened the kiss, and his tongue moved past the ridges on her teeth to meet hers. He—

Just then Carrie wrenched her mouth from his and tore out of his arms. Not even looking at him, she stammered, "I—I have to…" Then, wiping her mouth, she ran across the patio toward the house.

Jim stood there, dazed.

"Damn!" he muttered. He'd told himself to play it cool. And that kiss was anything *but* cool. He never should have kissed Carrie. They were co-workers. And apparently that was all they ever would be. Besides, hadn't he proven to himself that he was a jinx to anyone he loved?

Cursing under his breath, he gathered together any excuses he could muster. Excuses that Carrie would believe, which rather limited his choices. Finally, he set-tled on a modified version of the truth. It was a roman-tic moment and he'd kissed her on impulse. Then he'd add an apology.

He found her in the kitchen with Betty and Peter. "Is this a private affair?"

Peter and Betty immediately invited him to join them, but Carrie said an emphatic yes.

He licked his lips, trying to erase the pleasure her lips had given him. "Uh, Carrie, could I see you for a minute?"

"I'm busy," she said, suddenly stacking dishes.

"It's all right, child. I'll do it," Betty insisted, push-ing Carrie away.

"You can come right back in and help Betty. I won't take but a minute, I promise," said Jim.

Carrie kept her head down and walked into the hall-way in full sight of other guests.

"I owe you an apology. It was a romantic moment and I followed my instincts and I was wrong. It won't happen again."

Carrie muttered a thank-you, but she didn't look at him. Instead, she turned and went back into the kitchen.

Jim stared at the door she'd entered, but he didn't bother to open it. She'd made it clear she didn't want to discuss their kiss at all.

All he could hope was that she would put it out of her mind. And he'd pray he could do so, too. Otherwise, being around Carrie, who always looked sexy to him, would be a misery he might not be able to bear.

Vanessa's voice called him out of his thoughts. She was coming down the hall toward him.

She didn't look herself. "Are you okay?" he asked.

"Fine," she said, but it didn't sound like she meant it. "Trevor keeps following me around."

"Want me to get rid of him for you?"

"Can you do that?" she asked, a look of pleasure dawning on her face.

"I'll go talk to him," Jim said. Then, looking over Vanessa's shoulder, he said, "Here he is now."

"Vanessa, you listen to me!" Trevor exclaimed, ignoring Jim. "You owe me!"

"I don't owe you anything!" she exclaimed in return.

"Listen, you bitch, you led me on!"

Before he knew what was happening to him, Trevor found himself pressed up against the wall, an arm across his windpipe.

He struggled to protest, but Jim didn't allow him any air.

"You don't come into my sister's house and call her ugly names. And she owes you nothing. Understand?"

When Trevor nodded, Jim released him. "Apologize to her."

Instead, Trevor made the mistake of trying to smash Jim in the face. He found himself flat on the floor, not knowing what happened.

"Who did he come with?" Jim asked.

"Graham. I'll get him," Vanessa said, and hurried off to find him.

When Graham arrived, Jim released his hold on Trevor and helped him to his feet. "I think your friend is ready to go. And be sure you don't bring him back here again. He won't be welcome."

Graham took one look at Jim's glare and grabbed his protesting friend and dragged him out the door.

Vanessa looked at her brother, impressed with what he'd done. "My, I didn't realize all the advantages of having a big brother."

"I'm glad I was here. But you need to be careful who you associate with."

"But I hadn't heard anything bad about Trevor," Vanessa said, her eyes wide.

"I know, but be sure you know more about someone before you go on a date with him."

"Yes, Jim, and thanks again," she said with a smile.

"You're welcome, but don't take any calls from that guy, either. It won't take much encouragement before he thinks you owe him again. That kind of guy always blames you for whatever happens."

"Okay," Vanessa agreed, and hugged her brother.

Carrie came out of the kitchen to bump into them.

"Sorry, I didn't see you," she said, smiling at Vanessa.

"That's all right. I was just thanking Jim for getting rid of Trevor," Vanessa said.

"He became a problem?"

Vanessa recounted the action.

"Were there witnesses?" Carrie asked quickly.

"Witnesses?" Vanessa asked, puzzled by her question.

"The man has money. He'll try to sue because it will make up for feeling that he's been insulted."

"But it was his fault!" Vanessa exclaimed.

"Doesn't matter. Who was around?"

Vanessa named several people who were in the dining room or in the hallway. Carrie went to find them, hoping to get them to write a brief summation of the event, so they would have witnesses lined up.

"Do you think she's right?" Vanessa asked Jim.

"Yeah, unfortunately. After the party you'd better write things down before you forget, too."

"I'll do it right now," Vanessa said, turning to go into the kitchen.

Jim stood there, his head down, for a minute, then he went up the stairs and knocked on Will and Vivian's door. Will answered the door, a surprised look on his face.

"We had a bit of a problem downstairs, and I thought I should tell you about it," Jim said, his voice lowered.

Will slipped out and closed the door behind him. "Sorry, but Vivian is sleeping. Can we go down to the library?"

"Yeah, that would be good."

When the two men reached the library, Jim told Will what happened. Then he mentioned Carrie's belief that they should get statements from any witnesses at once.

"Good thinking. That girl's got a head on her shoulders."

"Yeah. Uh, Will, Vanessa's never taken a self-defense course. I think that would be a good idea."

"She hasn't? I never thought to ask. I know Carrie took one when she started to work for me. Then she went on and took some judo, too."

"Glad to know that," Jim said. "I had a feeling she could handle most anything." In fact, the woman was quite impressive. The longer he was around her, he realized Carrie might not need protecting, after all.

He told Will, "I'll go find Carrie and see if she needs any help."

"And I'll go check on Vanessa."

When Jim found Carrie, she was talking to several young ladies. He stepped up to them, and she introduced him. Apparently he hadn't met all the guests.

"Did they see what happened?"

"Yes, they had just left the dining room and turned around when they heard Trevor yelling. Ladies, can we go to the library and let you write a quick version of what you saw? Just in case Trevor decides to present a different version?"

"Sure, we'll do that," one woman said. "After all, it was all his fault."

"Come with me," Carrie said, ignoring Jim.

"Will may be in there. I—I asked him to come down."

Carrie glared at him, but she only nodded.

Jim stood there, staring as Carrie walked away from him…again.

CARRIE WAS SO GLAD the party was over.

The last guests had departed a few minutes ago. Except for Jim. She didn't know why he was still here. Then she corrected herself. Of course he was still here. He was family.

Jim, Will and Vanessa were talking in the library. She could join them, but she saw no reason. She hadn't seen the argument, only seen the results of it. She went upstairs to Vanessa's room and changed out of her party dress. Then she packed the things she'd brought with her and came back down the stairs.

She was tempted to leave without saying goodbye, but she knew that would be rude. Rapping on the door of the library, she immediately opened the door and stuck her head in.

"Carrie, come on in," Will said.

"No, I'm going home. I just wanted to let you know I'm leaving."

Jim immediately stood. "I'll go, too," he said.

"There's no need," she retorted, and walked out.

She'd made it to the front door when Jim caught up with her.

"What's your hurry?" he asked.

"I'm tired and ready to go home. What's yours?"

"I thought I'd follow you home, make sure you got there all right."

Carrie gave him an exasperated look. "I've managed to go home alone most of my life, Jim. Nothing's changed in the past few weeks that would require your escort."

"Maybe not," he agreed with a smile, "but we're going in the same direction, so why not?"

She glared at him and said, "Because you're not my big brother." She headed to her car, determined to ignore him.

On the ride home she was followed by Jim's headlights, taunting her and egging on her anger.

When was he going to get through his thick skull that she didn't need a keeper? She'd been on her own for a while and she'd done just fine, thank you very much, without Jim Barlow's watchful eye. That was a by-product of being on your own, she thought. Self-reliance.

Ever since Jim came to Dallas, she'd been feeling stressed, tense. She needed to start jogging again. To-morrow. Usually she jogged three or four times a week, but somehow, since Jim arrived, she'd been too distracted...or something. She needed to rev up her self-discipline.

Temptation seemed to be winning lately.

JIM WAS UP at his usual time, six-thirty. Ever since he'd moved into his apartment, he ran every morning. A re-sidual of the physical fitness regimen from the military.

He put on his running clothes, an old T-shirt from the marines and a pair of khaki-green shorts, and laced up his athletic shoes. Then he picked up his keys and went out his door, locking it behind him.

Once he reached the parking lot, he stretched a few times and began a slow jog, heading for the nearby park where he usually ran. By the time he reached the park, he was moving quickly, thinking about the night before and the events that had caused some problems. Head of the list was his kiss. How could something so wrong have felt so right?

Suddenly, he noted another runner. He'd never en-countered anyone on his morning jogs. The other jog-ger was far ahead of him and Jim sped up, interested in checking out the new person. When the sunshine caught on blond hair, and he was close enough to determine the runner was a female, his heart began to race faster.

Did Carrie jog?

But she'd been up late last night. They hadn't gotten home until almost one. Why would she pick today to start running? His gaze traveled up and down her body and he realized she was in good shape, whoever she was. This wasn't the first time she'd run.

"Carrie?" he called as he got closer.

The sharp turn of her head confirmed his guess. He raced to catch up with her. She continued to run, not slowing down for him. He wasn't surprised.

He managed to catch up with her. "I didn't know you jogged."

Sounding a little winded, she said, "I haven't been lately, but I need to keep in shape."

"We can jog together. I go every morning."

She didn't say anything.

"It will be safer for you if you jog with me," he pointed out.

All he got was a glare.

"I didn't mean you needed protection, Carrie. I just thought we could be company for each other."

She didn't respond, but she slowed down to a brisk walk. "I'm out of shape, Jim. I doubt that I can keep up with you."

Jim settled in beside her. "Last night I talked to Vanessa about her taking a self-defense course. I won't always be around to protect her."

"I think it's a good idea," Carrie said crisply, and started jogging again.

Jim said nothing else, but he adjusted his stride to run beside her, keeping pace with ease.

After two more rounds of the park, which was at least two miles, Carrie headed to the apartment at a walk. "I've had enough for the day. I'll see you at work."

Jim made another round of the park at a faster pace, but he scarcely noticed the distance. His mind was focused on Carrie.

She was an amazing young woman. He shouldn't have been surprised that she jogged, but she looked so innocent, so quiet, so unassuming. But the longer he knew her, the more he understood what a…complete woman she was. Her beauty was obvious, though she didn't play it up. Her brain was even more impressive.

Her physical skills finished the package. He'd met some impressive women in the marines, but never one like Carrie. Or maybe she just appealed to him more. She was a worthy partner in their work.

He didn't see her even once for the rest of the weekend. It was almost as if she was trying to hide from him.

When he reached the office Monday morning, Carrie was at her desk, looking like she never broke a sweat.

"Everything okay?" he asked.

"Yes, of course." She didn't look up. She never did. Never flirted with him, never indicated she liked his company.

Basically she acted like he didn't exist. Which should have pleased him. After all, he didn't want her to cling to him just because he'd kissed her. But he really didn't want her to act like the kiss hadn't affected her. It sure as hell had affected him.

He looked at those soft lips now. Only when she turned and glared at him did he realize he'd been staring.

"Did you want something?" she asked in irritation.

"No, sorry. I was just thinking about one of my cases."

Another few minutes passed in silence. Then Jim asked, "Have you heard from Will this morning?"

"Yes, he called. He said he'd be here a little late."

"I guess it's too early to think he might've heard from Trevor."

"I don't know. It depends how mad he was after Friday night and whom he could complain to."

"We know he has money. We know he's spoiled by his father. I wouldn't be surprised to find he got his father out of bed."

"It shouldn't be a problem. Any reputable lawyer wouldn't pursue the case once they saw the statements we took."

"Yeah. I don't think I thanked you Friday night, but you were right on target."

"No need to thank me."

She turned back to her work and Jim couldn't think of anything else to say. They worked in silence for another hour.

Will finally came in a little before eleven.

"Sorry I'm so late. I figured Trevor would try something, but I didn't think he'd be as fast as he was. What he said happened was quite different from every other telling of the events. Good thing we had those statements, Carrie. I took them to the lawyer who notified me this morning that they were filing a suit against Vanessa, her brother and me as owner of the house where the events took place."

Jim studied his partner. "What did you do?"

"I went to his office and showed him the statements we'd taken. He tried to bluff, saying his client had witnesses. I told him I didn't think that was possible. He's promised to talk to his client again to see if he'll reconsider the suit."

"Is he a good lawyer?" Jim asked.

"Yeah, he doesn't want to look like a fool. I'm pretty sure he won't touch this case. If Trevor does file suit, he'll have to find another lawyer."

"That won't be a problem since they're a dime a dozen," Jim muttered.

"Doesn't matter," Carrie said calmly. "The statements will show that Trevor's version is false and I doubt they can round up witnesses that will challenge what we have. After all, there was a limited guest list and most of them were close friends of Vanessa."

"Exactly," Will said. "So we put it behind us and keep working. So where are we on the Riley case?"

"Exactly where we were on Friday," Carrie said. "Riley and his wife are going to Vegas this Friday. They're staying at the Bellagio Hotel."

"Good taste in hotels, at least," Will said. "I think it's time for you two to make reservations, too."

"No!" Carrie protested. "I can do this alone."

"Carrie, this is a big job. For the sake of our company, we have to be sure to close the deal. This is the reason, other than being behind, that I wanted someone else to work with us. I don't want to leave town with Vivian and Danny here."

Carrie dropped her head, and Jim watched her, wondering if she would continue to fight his involvement. But when Will told them to make reservations on an earlier flight so that they'd already be in the hotel when the

Rileys arrived, all she said was "Jim and I will get together and decide. Then he'll call the hotel. I've already called pretending to be Mrs. Riley. We don't want to slip up there."

"Good. Okay, I'll leave it up to the two of you," Will said. "Oh, and if we hear any more about a lawsuit, I'll bring Jeff in on it."

"Oh, yeah, I forgot Rebecca's husband was a lawyer." Jim's mind was on going to Vegas with Carrie, more than a senseless lawsuit.

Excitement ran through his veins, which made him chastise himself. After all, he wasn't a kid. He was a professional. But all he could think about was going to Vegas with Carrie.

Chapter Fourteen

Carrie hoped to stall the discussion with Jim until she'd had time to gather her defenses. But he wanted to talk as soon as Will left them alone.

"I don't see much to decide, Carrie. We have to be settled into the hotel before they get there. Do you know their flight number?"

"After talking to Susie and checking all the flights to Vegas, they're either on the 12:15 p.m. flight on American, or there's a flight that goes to Albuquerque and then Vegas that leaves fifteen minutes later."

"I should think they'd take the direct flight," Jim said, frowning.

"I'm not sure. They might prefer the Albuquerque flight because they'll think no one is following them unless they're on both flights."

"Good thinking. So when should we leave?"

"If we take the 7:45 a.m. flight, we'll get there at least four hours ahead of time. We can pay extra and check into our room when we arrive. We'll make the reservation for the weekend, checking out on Monday morning, but if we get what we need, we'll come back early. Is that okay with you?"

"Sure, that will be fine. So shall I use my real name for the reservation?"

"Yes, they haven't had any contact with you. That will be fine." Carrie turned away. She'd done what she had to do. Dwelling on what would happen over the next weekend was useless.

A couple of minutes later, Jim informed her that he'd gotten their reservation for the Bellagio. Then he cleared his throat.

She was learning to read him. That sound meant there was more to the story. "What else?"

"Well, they—they were full, except for one of their bridal suites. So I told them we were newlyweds."

"You what?" Carrie exclaimed loudly enough to bring Will to the door of his office.

"What's wrong?" he asked, staring at Carrie.

Unable to put together a coherent sentence, she waved toward Jim.

"I, uh, the hotel didn't have a vacancy in their regular rooms. They only had a bridal suite open and I told them—" He broke off and snatched a quick look at Carrie before he turned back to Will. "I told them we were newlyweds."

"Good decision," Will agreed. "Guess you'll need some new clothes, Carrie. Every bride would have them. Remember, the only way to carry out a deception is to pay attention to details. Take some time off and go shopping, why don't you?"

Carrie gulped and then calmly looked at Will and

said, "I don't need to shop, Will, but I could use some time off today," she said without any emotion.

Jim immediately said, "Maybe I should escort you to the mall, Carrie. I'm sure you can find something—"

"Don't push it, Barlow!"

Jim backed off.

Carrie, her spine stiff, rose from her chair. "In fact, I'll go now. I'm sure you won't mind watching the phones, Jim."

After the door closed behind her, Will looked at Jim. "I guess that was payback, huh?"

"I guess so, but I don't mind watching the phones. And at lunchtime I can go get us some sandwiches and we can eat here, if you want."

"Good idea," Will said. "Carrie and I used to do that. We did most of our talking over lunch."

Jim frowned. "Maybe she misses that. Tomorrow I should offer to bring back lunch. I hadn't realized my joining you would cause so many changes."

Will leaned against the doorjamb. "I hadn't thought of that, but I guess my eating with you most days has made a difference in Carrie's day. But usually that happens when Vanessa comes to have lunch with Carrie."

"Yeah. By the way, you know I encouraged Vanessa to take self-defense lessons. I got the name of the place where Carrie went. Why didn't Vanessa go with Carrie?"

"It was right after Carrie's father's death. She had cut herself off from Vanessa and I hadn't met Vivian or Vanessa yet. It really pleased both of them when Carrie came back into Vanessa's life."

"I guess so. It took me a while to figure out why they were friends."

"What do you mean?" Will asked, sitting down in Carrie's chair.

"Wealthy people don't usually form friendships with people who don't have money."

Will smiled. "Yeah, that's what I thought, too. Until I met Vivian."

"She does seem different."

"Yeah, she wanted to adopt all of you when she found out Vanessa had siblings. Herbert wouldn't consider such a thing."

"Carrie said something like that. I didn't think she was serious." Jim shuffled some papers.

"Vivian was serious about it. At the time she was only twenty and definitely under Herbert's thumb. Back when a woman accepted her husband's decisions without protest. Fortunately, women aren't taught to obey their husbands anymore."

"Even if they were, Carrie wouldn't," Jim said with a grin. "She's a fighter."

"She had to be or she wouldn't have survived when her life was shattered after her father died," Will said solemnly.

"I know. I have that troubled background more in common with Carrie than with Vanessa. We've both faced hard times."

Will fiddled with one of Carrie's pens. "I hadn't thought about that, but it's true. I guess you're well suited to each other."

"As workers," Jim hurriedly said.

Will studied his face. "Only as workers?"

"I told you, Will, I'm a jinx."

"I thought we'd agreed that logic dispelled that belief." Will watched him.

"Nice try, but I don't think so."

CARRIE WENT BACK to her apartment and changed into jogging clothes. She hadn't gone out that morning because she hadn't wanted to run into Jim. Now she could jog without that fear.

And she needed to calm down.

Thoughts of spending the weekend in Vegas with Jim, pretending to be newlyweds, was a little overwhelming. She needed to rebuild her defenses. If it was possible.

She'd been unsettled ever since Jim's kiss Friday night. It had been so sweet, so dreamy. She almost snorted at her sappy thought. Life wasn't dreamy! She knew that because of her past. She had to force herself to face reality.

The reality was as Jim had explained. It had been a romantic moment. He was a man. A man responded to sexual opportunity.

Not that Jim had gone beyond what was acceptable. No, unfortunately, he'd left Carrie wanting more. She'd been fighting that feeling ever since.

Damn it! She wasn't being honest. She'd been fighting that feeling ever since Jim had walked into the office that first day.

Carrie began running faster, as if trying to outrun her thoughts. She needed to leave those thoughts behind, or the trip to Vegas would be a disaster.

She spent the rest of the day doing errands, including grocery shopping and a trip to the post office. The stores were open until nine every night. She wasn't going to tell Will that, but she could do any shopping she needed in the evenings.

Later, as she was preparing her dinner, a knock on her door surprised her. She went to the door and looked through the peephole, then slowly opened it.

"Yes, Jim?"

"Just thought I'd check to see if your shopping was successful."

"Not really."

"Oh. Are you going to run in the morning?"

"I don't know. I guess it depends on what time I get up."

Jim grinned at her. "I could offer to wake you up."

"No, thanks."

He looked over her head and sniffed the air. "Something smells good."

Carrie knew he'd like her to invite him to dinner, but she fought the urge to do as he wanted. "Yes, I'm cooking."

"Will and I were talking today and he mentioned that you used to go pick up lunch for the two of you and you'd talk over lunch."

She cautiously agreed. "Yes."

"I thought I'd pick up lunch for the three of us tomorrow and we could visit while we ate."

"I don't mind watching the office while you and Will go out to eat," she said abruptly.

"There's no reason you should, though. We're all partners, aren't we?"

"Yes, but—"

"Let's just try it tomorrow. We'll see how it goes. We could schedule it at least once a week."

"I suppose so." Before he could suggest anything else, Carrie looked over her shoulder. "I have to take my supper off the stove," she said hurriedly.

"Go ahead," Jim said, and stepped into the apartment.

Carrie backed away, frustrated that she hadn't handled the situation better and gotten Jim out of her apartment.

She took the pasta off the stove and drained it.

"Ah, you're having pasta? I love pasta."

Carrie ground her teeth. Then, after drawing a deep breath, she said, "I can give you some to take home with you."

"That's not necessary. I just thought— I don't like to eat alone."

Carrie gave up. "Sit down, Jim. Dinner will be ready in a couple of minutes."

"Thanks, Carrie. Is there anything I can do?"

"Yes, pour some iced tea you'll find in the refrigerator."

She added to the salad and put it on the table. Then she put out more silverware. She poured the sauce on the pasta and put it in a serving dish. Jim, holding two filled glasses, reached the table.

"Wow, this looks great, Carrie."

"It's very simple."

As they ate, Jim brought up a variety of subjects for conversation. Carrie knew he was intentionally trying to take her mind off his presence, and it worked...to an extent. She actually enjoyed the meal. But she never forgot Jim was sitting at her table.

After they finished eating, he insisted on helping her do the dishes, which took all of five minutes. When they finished, he suggested they watch television for a little while, but she refused, telling him she had some errands to run.

"Then I guess I should go and get out of your way," he said with a smile.

"Sorry. Maybe another time," she said, keeping her gaze down.

His hand lifted her chin up. "Thanks for the dinner, Carrie. I enjoyed it a lot. After we get back from Vegas, I'll pay you back by taking you out to dinner."

"That's not necessary," she assured him, pulling away from his hold. She moved to the door and opened it.

Jim walked through, thanking her again before she could shut the door.

She fell against the closed door, regretting she'd rushed him away. But she had no choice. If they'd remained together, she might let herself lose control.

Which brought her back to thoughts of Vegas.

If she couldn't handle one small meal, how the heck would she survive a weekend with him in a honeymoon suite?

WILL LOOKED AT VANESSA as they ate dinner that night. "Did you sign up for your self-defense class?"

"I did. But I wish I didn't have to take it by myself."

"I'll take it with you," Vivian said, surprising both her husband and her daughter.

Will reached out his hand to his wife. "Vivian, I'm here to protect you."

"Of course you are, dear, but you're not with me all the time. I've never worried about it since Herbert died because Vanessa was an adult by then. But now with Danny... He couldn't take care of himself if something happened to me in the next twenty years."

"But, Mom, I'd take care of him," Vanessa put in. "And so would Will."

"I know that, but wouldn't it be better if I have some idea of how to protect myself so that situation doesn't arise?"

"Yes, of course," Will agreed. "But do you feel fit enough after Danny's birth?"

"Of course I do," she said, giving him a challenging look, daring him to disagree.

Will didn't. "I guess that takes care of that problem, Vanessa. Sign your mother up for that class, too."

"Okay. By the way, did our matchmaking work on Jim and Carrie?"

Will grimaced. "There's something between them, but Jim feels he's a jinx to anyone he loves. He doesn't intend to have a relationship with anyone."

"Did he lose someone he loved?" Vanessa asked.

Vivian said, "Think, child."

"You mean our parents? But that wasn't his fault. And Wally was killed in war!"

"Apparently there was a young woman he loved and she was killed in an accident a few days after he shipped out," Will explained.

"He wasn't even there!" Vanessa almost shouted.

"I pointed out the lack of logic in his fears, but he said I hadn't convinced him. That's why he was so reluctant to come to the hospital the night Jamie was born." Will added, "He said it was a real relief that the baby was healthy."

"But what can we do? We can't let him go to waste!"

"He's not a crop to be harvested," Vivian protested.

"No, he's much more important. He's a good man, and they're hard to find. And Carrie needs a good man. It would be so perfect!"

"I think we're making progress," Will said calmly.

"What do you mean?" Vanessa asked.

"They're going on a honeymoon to Vegas."

"They're getting married?" Vanessa exclaimed joyously.

"No, Vanessa. I said they were going on a honeymoon. I didn't mention marriage."

Vivian put down her fork. "I think you need to explain yourself, Will Greenfield! I won't have Carrie mistreated!"

"Neither would I, my love," Will said with a grin. He explained all about the case they were working on and how they were sharing the bridal suite.

"How did Carrie accept that situation?" Vivian asked.

"She's upset, but she knows it's necessary. Anything else that happens is between the two of them."

"But she might not want—"

"You know Jim. Do you believe he would continue if Carrie said no?" Will shook his head. "And after all, Carrie has taken that self-defense class. She might not be able to win against Jim, but she damn sure wouldn't stop trying."

"You're right, dear," Vivian said with a small smile.

"Does Carrie know how Jim feels?" Vanessa asked. "I mean about feeling guilty for the deaths in his life?"

"I doubt it."

"Hmm," Vanessa said, the wheels obviously turning in her head.

JUST AS JIM GOT UP to go get lunch for the three of them the next day, Vanessa strolled into the office.

"Hello, everybody!"

Jim and Carrie greeted her, and Will came out of his office. "Hi, there, Vanessa. What are you doing here?"

"I know it's short notice, but I need to borrow Carrie for lunch."

"But we were going to have lunch together," Jim exclaimed.

"You and Carrie?" Vanessa asked in surprise.

"No, the three of us," Jim explained.

"Couldn't you do that tomorrow? I want to have lunch with Carrie today."

Jim just stared at his sister, unable to answer.

"Is that okay with you, Carrie?" Will asked. "Actually that might be better because we can go over last-minute preparations for your trip this weekend."

"Yes, that's fine," Carrie hurriedly said. She grabbed her purse and went out the door with Vanessa.

Jim didn't speak until the two ladies had disappeared. Then he said, "My little sister is slightly spoiled, Will. You'll have to agree with that."

"Absolutely," Will said with a smile. "But, like her mother, she has a good heart."

ONCE THEY WERE SEATED in the restaurant, Carrie looked at her friend. "What was so important that you insisted on lunch today?"

Vanessa slumped in her chair. "My party was useless."

"What do you mean?" Carrie asked, leaning toward Vanessa.

"There's no use in me trying to find a lady for Jim. He's not interested."

Carrie stared at her friend, shock on her face. "Are you telling me Jim's gay? I don't believe it!"

"No, not that. But he thinks he's a jinx to anyone he gets close to." She then went on to repeat what Will had told her.

"That's terrible," Carrie muttered. "He said something to me about his parents and Wally dying, but I didn't really understand. No wonder he wanted to dance with me at the party. He was trying to avoid any women he might feel attracted to."

"Oh, I don't think that's true," Vanessa hurriedly said. "I'm sure it's because he's attracted to you."

"Me? Don't be ridiculous, Vanessa. And even if he was, it wouldn't matter since he doesn't plan on getting close to anyone of the female persuasion."

"I was hoping you could tempt him," Vanessa said in a mischievous voice.

Carrie was horrified. "Vanessa! What are you suggesting?"

Chapter Fifteen

Thursday's lunch was a group affair at the office. Jim went out and bought sandwiches and the three of them gathered around Will's desk for their noon meal.

"Pass me the potato chips," Will requested.

The bag was passed to him and he put some on his paper plate. "This is great. It's like a picnic."

Jim eyed his partner. "Yeah. You haven't had enough picnics?"

"No. Betty doesn't think picnics are proper meals. I don't dare tell her we brought in food for lunch. She'd think I needed twice as much to eat for dinner."

"We won't tell," Carrie assured him.

"I don't know," Jim said in a considering voice. "I might be interested in blackmail. Or maybe a dinner invitation."

"Done," Will agreed with a big grin. "You have an open invitation."

"Maybe I'll take you up on that after we get back from Vegas," Jim said. "I've made a copy of our itinerary in case you need to find us. Plus, we'll have our cells."

"What cameras are you taking with you?" Will asked.

"I'll have my digital camera with me, and my camera phone," Carrie said.

"I'm taking a small camera in this pen," Jim said, holding up what looked like a ballpoint pen. "I'll have to be close for it to work, but that might happen."

Will nodded. "All right. And remember to begin your cover from the moment you leave your apartment, you two. You never know who you'll run into, or what they'll say that might expose your secret."

"Right," Jim agreed. "Wedding rings from the word go."

"Yeah. You've got those, right?"

They both nodded.

"Do you know anything about Riley's gambling habits?" Will asked.

"Some," Carrie said. "He usually plays blackjack, but he also likes craps and roulette."

"And Mrs. Riley?"

"She likes the slots," Carrie said.

"How are you two going to work that?"

"We'll stay together," Jim said. "Mrs. Riley's not scamming the insurance company so we'll stick to Mr. Riley. Occasionally one of us will go play some slots, just to locate the wife and make sure she won't notice us taking pictures whenever Riley leaves the gaming tables."

"Good. Now, I'm going to the bank after lunch. Have you figured out how much cash you'll need?"

Jim and Will discussed the proper amount, but Carrie didn't concern herself with their discussion. She knew she could turn in an expense account after her return and get her money reimbursed. Instead, she was mentally reviewing the clothes she would pack that evening.

She tended to buy unnoticeable clothes that allowed her to blend in with the scenery, which was helpful in her job. But they wouldn't work on this trip. No. On this trip she needed sexier clothes. Clothes a bride would wear to entice her new husband.

"Carrie?"

She jerked her head up and stared at Will. "Yes?"

"I called you several times. What were you thinking about?"

"The trip. Trying to make sure I had all my ducks in a row, that's all." She ignored Jim's sharp look. The last thing she needed was for Jim to start reading her mind.

"Any problems?" he asked.

"No, of course not," she hurriedly said. "Everything's fine."

But would she say that once she got to Vegas?

THAT NIGHT, Carrie packed her clothes. She put in some bright-colored tops and some sexy underwear. She was supposed to be a newlywed, after all. She'd even bought a couple of nightgowns.

The one thing she'd bought that she hadn't told Jim about was in a box in her bathroom, awaiting her. She didn't really like using it, but because she'd seen Mrs. Riley before, she couldn't take a chance that she might recognize her.

The next morning, when Jim knocked on her door, Carrie swung it open and waited for his reaction.

"What happened to the good-looking blonde who lives here?" he demanded, staring at her brown hair.

"She's in disguise," Carrie whispered. Then she picked up her suitcase and purse and entered the hallway so she could lock her apartment door.

"Here, I'll take that," Jim said, reaching out for her bag. "I've already taken mine down to the car. Why did you dye your hair?"

"It's just a rinse to last for the weekend. I was afraid Mrs. Riley might recognize me if I didn't do something to my hair."

"Maybe. But you were wearing heavy makeup when you went to her house."

"I'm wearing makeup now," Carrie returned, annoyed that he hadn't noticed.

"Yeah, I can tell, but that day you wore too much."

As much as his words irritated her, she knew he was right. "Let's go," she said firmly.

"Right this way, dear wife," he said, gesturing for her to precede him.

There was little conversation on the way to the airport, but once he'd parked the car, Jim said, "Okay, from here until our return, we're married. Remember?"

"I think I've been doing this longer than you," she pointed out.

"Good. Give me a kiss."

"What?"

"Brides like to kiss their husbands…frequently." He leaned toward her.

Carrie knew he was right and she had to pretend. She closed her eyes and puckered up.

His lips brushed hers and her eyes popped open.

"Okay, now let's go."

Jim shook his head but said nothing. He got out of his car and took both their suitcases out of the vehicle. "Ready?"

"Yes." She followed him from the parking lot into the terminal, where they checked their bags and went to the gate to await their flight. When Jim caught her hand, she didn't protest, though she thought he might be overdoing it just a little.

Until she saw the Rileys sitting at the gate.

Suddenly she turned toward Jim, throwing her arms around his neck and putting her lips against his neck as she quietly whispered, "They're here."

Jim wrapped his arms around her. "Where?" he whispered.

"In the second row of seats to your right."

"Okay, I'm going to keep my arm around you and take us up to the desk to be sure we get seats together." He kissed her cheek and did as he said.

She kept an arm around his waist, clinging as a newlywed would do. After receiving their seat assignments, Jim led them to the row of seats behind the Rileys and several seats down from them.

Jim was quite solicitous and Carrie played along. She put her head on his shoulder.

"Tired, sweetheart? I guess I didn't let you get much sleep last night."

"I'm just a little sleepy."

"Once we get on the plane, you can put your head on my shoulder and sleep all the way to Vegas."

"Mmm, I can't wait," she whispered.

Jim hugged her close and kissed her again.

And that was the scariest part of their pretense. She could get used to touching and being touched by this man.

When they got off the plane in Vegas, after Carrie had actually slept a little with her head on Jim's shoulder, they took a cab to the Bellagio. They noted that the Rileys were met by a white stretch limo.

"Some people spend their money in a hurry," he whispered in her ear as the taxi pulled away.

She lay her head on his shoulder again and didn't respond. She'd noted that Riley was still using his wheelchair. What if he stuck with it the entire trip and their efforts were wasted?

Their taxi actually got them to the hotel faster than the Rileys' limo. She and Jim were checking in when the Rileys came through the door.

Carrie grabbed Jim's muscular arm and leaned closer to him. "He's not in the wheelchair."

Jim, to his credit, didn't look over his shoulder. He took the key the desk clerk handed him and turned to put an arm around Carrie. "Come on, sweetheart."

"What about our bags?"

"The bellhop will bring them." He leaned down and kissed her briefly. Then he pulled her right past the Rileys toward the elevator.

When they reached the bridal suite, Jim opened the door and then scooped Carrie up into his arms and stepped across the threshold.

Held against his rock-hard chest, she felt as if she didn't breathe until he put her down to tip the bellhop.

When she heard him close the door, she finally let out the emotion she'd been hiding since they'd encountered the Riley's in the Dallas airport.

"I don't know how I got their flight information wrong. From what Susie said, I was sure they'd be on a later flight."

"Don't beat yourself up over it, Carrie. It's just as well."

"Yeah, well let's hope that's our first and last mistake of this trip." She looked around the suite. They were standing in the living room portion, and beyond double doors she could see the bedroom with a giant-size bed layered with luxurious red linens. Well, it was a honeymoon suite, she reasoned. Tearing her eyes away from that room, she spun around. "Shall we head for the casino? I'm sure the Rileys will."

Jim grinned. "Anxious to get out of here?"

Had he read her mind? Instead of admitting it, she hedged, "I just thought—"

"I know, honey, but newlyweds wouldn't go to the casino first thing. They'd choose another activity first."

Carrie understood what he was saying, but she had no intention of indulging in sex for an hour or two. Much as she might like to.

As if he read her mind, he said, "No, I'm not suggesting we make love, dear heart. I'm suggesting we pretend. Come on."

She swallowed, and then followed him into the bedroom. What did he have in mind?

He took off his shoes and crawled onto the big bed. "Come on."

"Why?"

"So housekeeping can talk about how the newly-weds couldn't wait to get into bed," he assured her, leaning on one elbow. "If you want, you can take a little nap to make up for the early morning. I think I will."

He flopped back onto one of the pillows and closed his eyes, as if what she did meant nothing to him.

After a moment, Carrie kicked off her shoes and gingerly got onto the big bed. She was tired, she admitted, and a little sleep would help.

Jim didn't move, which appeased Carrie's apprehension, and gradually she relaxed. Just as she was falling asleep, she felt strong arms gather her close to a warm body. She snuggled up and slept like a baby.

JIM AWOKE a couple of hours later, only to discover his arms around Carrie as she slept on his shoulder.

Not a bad way to wake up, he decided. Too bad it wasn't for real. If it were, he'd pull her closer and let her know how much he wanted her. She'd turn in his arms and give him a sexy smile right before she kissed him and gave herself to him.

Only in your dreams, Jim, he chided himself.

Instead, he eased his arms from around her and sat up, trying his hardest to bring his wanton desires in check.

Beside him, Carrie stirred. When she saw him sitting beside her, her eyes filled with something akin to fear and she jerked up as if she'd been stabbed in the back. "Oh! Is it time? Shall we go down?"

"Sure, when we're ready. I don't think there's any rush. We want to be sure we get the goods on Riley without taking any risks," Jim said.

"Of course," Carrie hurriedly agreed as she slid off the bed. She rushed into the bathroom and closed the door.

Jim sighed. Well, at least they'd gotten through that without a major embarrassment. But he wouldn't forget those minutes spent holding her.

Half an hour later, they descended to the casino for the first time. Carrie had a handbag on her shoulder that held both her camera and her digital camera. Jim had his pen camera. Of course, they both knew photos weren't allowed inside the casinos, so they'd have to catch Riley coming or going.

First they had to find the man.

As they began their tour of the casino, Carrie, her hand held by Jim, leaned over to whisper that she'd spotted Mrs. Riley at a bank of slot machines near the entrance.

Within minutes, they found Riley playing at a blackjack table, sitting on a high stool. There was no sign of his wheelchair, but they knew they'd have to get pictures of him on his feet for real proof.

Rather than join Riley's table, Jim took a seat at another blackjack table where he had a clear view of the subject. "Will you stay and watch me play, sweetheart?" he asked, putting an arm around Carrie.

"Of course, dear," Carrie cooed, then wondered if she'd overdone her response.

Jim didn't appear to think so. Carrie stood at his side. Her job was to keep an eye on Riley while Jim concentrated on his cards.

Several hours later, Jim cashed out and they wandered around, watching others play.

Jim whispered, "I can't believe the man has such staying power!"

Carrie gave a quiet chuckle. "He's obviously dedicated to his gambling." She'd kept track of Jim's gaming, also. He'd actually come out ahead.

"Let's try the craps table, shall we?" Jim suggested. "You can roll the dice for me for luck."

"Yes, but what kind?" she teased.

"It had better be good luck or we won't last long at this game."

Carrie rolled the dice and seemed to bring Jim luck. They got a little wrapped up in the game as Jim began to pile the chips up in front of him. They were both surprised when Riley joined their table.

They exchanged a look, but it was too late. Riley was already seated on a stool, placing his bet. After a few minutes, Carrie pleaded with Jim to quit. She said she was tired of rolling the dice.

He gave her money to go play the slots, but he remained at his seat.

Carrie wandered over to the slots where she saw Mrs. Riley was still plunking in the coins at her slot machine. After a while Carrie returned close to the craps table.

As if he realized someone was watching, Riley turned around and looked at the people behind him. Not wanting to be caught staring, Carrie approached Jim, telling him she wanted to go see a show.

With a shrug, he cashed in his chips and left the table. "I made enough to go to any show you want, Carrie," he whispered.

"That's good, I guess. I wish we would've gotten pictures of Riley, but I don't think he's leaving the casino anytime soon."

"Yeah, we'll try again later."

"I watched him for a few minutes at the craps table, but he must've sensed something, because that's when he turned around."

"I know, and that's why I left the table. Better not to push it today. We've got time."

Time? The word struck terror in her heart. Time meant more nights in that den of iniquity, otherwise known as the honeymoon suite. And after today's little escapade on the bed, time was the one thing Carrie didn't have much of.

AFTER SEEING the Cirque du Soleil show, they visited the casino again before going up to their room. Riley was at the tables and showed no signs of leaving.

When they reached the room, Carrie stepped away from Jim's touch. "I think I'll watch a little television," she said, switching on the set and sitting down on the couch.

"What's on?" Jim asked, as if the programming was terribly important to him. Without waiting for an answer, he settled beside her on the couch.

He sat close enough that their shoulders almost touched. Truth to tell, Carrie had enjoyed the evening with Jim holding her, being solicitous, acting like her husband. Withdrawal now was difficult.

Jim extended his arm along the back of the couch, behind her. "We worked well together today," he said.

"We didn't get the proof we needed."

"Maybe not. But we will. It's clear Riley thinks he's

in the clear here. There's been no sign of his wheelchair since he left the airport."

Carrie frowned. "He must've arranged to leave it in the limo. Maybe we should contact the limo driver and find out for sure."

"We could do that, but it's still not the proof we need in a picture."

"I guess so." Carrie sighed.

"You tired? My shoulder's available," Jim offered.

"No, I'm fine."

After another half hour of mindless comedy on television, Jim said, "Don't you think it's time to turn in?"

"I'm sure Riley won't be up early in the morning."

"Probably not, but I need my sleep."

"Go ahead. I like to watch the late-night shows." She hoped he'd go to sleep. Then she could snatch a pillow and a blanket and sleep on the sofa.

"So you'll come to bed later?" Jim asked, pushing her for an answer.

She didn't look at him. "I might sleep here on the sofa. It's quite comfortable."

"Go ahead and go to bed, Carrie. I'll take the sofa," he said with a sigh.

"No. I'm smaller than you. This will be fine for me. If you don't mind, I'll take a pillow and a blanket from the bed."

"Of course," he agreed, getting up and going to the bedroom.

Carrie followed, glad to have everything settled. She took the pillow and blanket from Jim and returned to the couch. Jim closed the door and she heaved a sigh of relief that she wouldn't see him again until morning.

THE NEXT MORNING she woke in Jim's arms as he carried her to the bedroom.

"Jim! What—"

"The hotel is bringing us breakfast as part of the service to the bridal suite. I thought it would look odd if they noticed you spent the night on the sofa."

"Oh yes, of course. My pillow?"

"I'll get it," he said, putting her on her feet in the bedroom. "Get in bed."

Carrie kicked off her shoes, and suddenly realized she was still wearing her clothes from last night. She hopped onto the high bed and brought the covers up to her neck.

Jim was shirtless when he returned with the pillow, but Carrie barely caught a glimpse of his naked chest before there was a knock at the door and he went to answer it.

Carrie heard him tell the room-service waiter to bring their breakfast to the dining table at one end of the living room.

"No, my wife will be out in a minute," Jim assured the waiter just before Carrie heard the outer door close. She got out of bed and peeked into the living room.

"Is it safe?" she asked.

He nodded. "I'll go put on a shirt. You go ahead and start eating."

She did no such thing, of course. Instead, she uncovered the dishes and filled their plates. Then she poured him a cup of coffee and made herself a cup of tea. "Ready?" she asked as he entered the room.

Jim looked at what she'd done. "Absolutely. I hope you have an appetite."

"I do." She waited until he was seated to begin eating.

Jim poured syrup on his pancakes and took a forkful. "This is even better than Betty's breakfasts, but I'll never tell her that."

Carrie agreed, though she hardly tasted anything she ate. She was still too preoccupied by the glimpse she'd caught of Jim's naked chest....

Chapter Sixteen

As they left their suite, Jim wrapped his arm around Carrie and pulled her close for a kiss. A kiss that stirred her all the way to her toes.

Then he whispered in her ear, "We have an audience."

Carrie's heart sank. For a moment she had forgotten their pretense.

With his arm around her, Jim led her to the elevators where another couple was waiting. They exchanged smiles and Jim said, "We're on our honeymoon."

"How wonderful," the woman said.

Her husband just nodded. Then he began talking about his gambling and Jim compared notes with him.

Carrie had already decided Vegas would be a terrible place for a honeymoon. Gambling seemed to be of prime importance to most of the people there. She thought an island in the sun where there was little in the way of organized activities would be her choice for a real honeymoon spot.

Jim gave her a squeeze, bringing her attention back

to their new friends. "Sorry, I was, uh, thinking. Did I miss something?"

"Mrs. Langford asked if you had done any shopping, honey."

"No, not really," she told the woman as they entered the elevator. "Jim likes to gamble and I've stayed close to him."

Mrs. Langford smiled at her. "Spoken like a true newlywed. Well, you two enjoy yourselves."

When Carrie and Jim made their way into the casino, they noticed Riley's wife at the slot machines. Carrie lingered in the area, until the woman gave up her place and headed toward the restaurants. Then she went to find Jim at the roulette table. Riley was sitting there, as well.

Coming up behind Jim, she slid her arms around his neck. "Miss me?" she whispered.

He turned and encircled her with his arms. "Sure did," he said, and added a kiss.

"Place your bet," the croupier called, and Jim hurriedly moved a stack of chips onto the table. When the ball settled, he discovered he'd doubled his bet.

"You bring me luck, babe." Jim patted her cheek.

The next few spins had the same results, and Jim's stack of chips grew, attracting Riley's attention from across the table.

"Your little lady is one good-luck charm," he called out.

Carrie smiled at him, then leaned down to hug Jim. "I have an idea. Go with it," she whispered in his ear. Then she said aloud, "I've got to go to the ladies' room. I'll be back soon, honey."

As she strode away from the table, Riley called her back, but Carrie ignored him. She went out to the lobby, picked up the house phone and dialed the front desk. Then she asked that they page her husband. He was in the casino and she had an emergency.

"And your husband's name, ma'am?"

"Richard Riley."

JIM PLACED another bet, but Riley went against him this time since his last bet, after Carrie's departure, had been a loser.

"Not betting with me anymore?" he asked with a grin.

"Naw. You start losing, I bet opposite of you. Keeps me on a win streak."

About that time, they heard a page for a Richard Riley to come to the lobby for an emergency phone call.

"Wonder who that poor guy is," Jim said.

"It's me. But I don't want to go. I might lose my place."

"But they said it was an emergency," Jim pointed out.

Riley grumbled, then gathered up his chips and reluctantly left the table. Walking.

Jim waited a couple of minutes before he followed him. When he reached the lobby, Carrie was putting away her camera and Riley was hurrying to her, anger on his face. Jim ran, but he still had some distance to make up. Before he could reach them, Riley grabbed Carrie's purse. Carrie immediately leaped from her chair and jabbed him in the ribs with her elbow. Then she landed a karate chop on his neck, knocking Riley to the floor, where he lay in a heap.

Several hotel personnel rushed to Carrie.

"What's going on?" one of them who'd identified himself as the manager asked.

"This man tried to get my purse," Carrie said in angry tones. "He thought he'd just pull it out of my hands and run."

"Security is on its way," the manager said just as Jim reached the group surrounding Carrie.

"What happened, honey?" Jim asked.

Carrie broke through the group and hugged Jim's neck, repeating what she'd already told the others.

"This is the man who sat with me in the casino. I guess he thought you took my winnings when you left," Jim said. "Are you all right?"

"I feel a little weak. Can we go to our room?" Carrie asked.

The manager took down their room number and agreed to send them a complimentary fruit basket to make her feel better.

When they reached their hotel room, Carrie immediately called Will and sent the pictures to their office via Jim's laptop so Will could forward the pictures on to the insurance company.

"I feel a little guilty about causing Riley so much trouble, but he has no right to bilk the insurance company," Carrie said.

"You handled everything beautifully. I was following, afraid you'd need some protection. Instead, you had the man on the floor in no time."

"I told you I could take care of myself, Jim. I don't need your protection like Vanessa does." She sat down on the sofa, now that she'd sent the pictures. "What do we do now?"

"I need to talk to the limo driver. Why don't you start packing? Oh, and you could call and switch our tickets to an evening flight."

She agreed to his requests. After he left, she picked up the phone to call the airline, but five minutes later she hung up the phone, frustrated. They couldn't fly out tonight. In fact, she got the last two tickets for an early-morning flight. So they had no choice but to stay in Vegas for one more night.

She immediately called Will to tell him they'd be back in the morning. He seemed cheerful enough, not worrying about the expense of another night in the hotel. "You and Jim have a good time, honey. You deserve it with those pictures you got. The insurance company was ecstatic."

After hanging up the phone, she bowed her head and prayed for strength to resist Jim's charms just another twelve or fifteen hours. At least until she was back at home. Then she could judge her abilities to resist him in normal circumstances.

A knock on the door brought her to her feet. Through the peephole, she saw one of the security guards standing there alone. She swung open the door. "Yes?"

"Ma'am, we've escorted Mr. Riley to his room and requested that he leave."

"Good. Thank you," she said, and began to close the door.

The guard reached out and stopped her, and she gave him a curious look.

He coughed and then said, "I think everything would

be fine if you erased the pictures in your camera. That seems to be the problem with Mr. Riley. Seems as you were snapping your photos in the lobby, you got him." He shrugged. "Some people are funny about their privacy. Anyway, he was just trying to get your camera away from you, not steal your purse."

"I see," she said calmly. "I could do that," she added after a moment.

"It might be better if you let me do it. Then I can assure Mr. Riley he has nothing to worry about."

"No, I'll erase them, but you can watch," she said with an innocent smile.

Jim arrived at the door. "What's going on?"

Carrie explained the situation to him as she got the camera.

"And you're willing to do that?" Jim asked cautiously.

"Of course, dear. Pictures of an unknown man aren't that exciting," she assured him with a smile. Then she turned to the security guard. "See? Here is my delete button. I just push it and…you can see the pictures are gone."

"Thanks, ma'am."

"No problem…" She read the name on his badge. "Mr. Boswell" Then she closed the door after him, a smile on her lips.

"I assume you're not upset?" Jim asked.

"No. I sent the pictures to Will, remember?"

"Yes, but what if the transmission didn't go through? It could be—"

"I talked to Will. He's already spoken to someone at the insurance company who received the pictures and was ecstatic about them."

"So I guess the only thing left to do is to get the hell out of Dodge."

"Not if you intend to fly," she said softly. "The airlines are booked. I couldn't get us any tickets until tomorrow morning. The flight leaves at eight." She turned away when she saw the disappointment on his face.

With what sounded like forced cheerfulness to Carrie, Jim said, "Well, I guess we'll just have to enjoy ourselves for a few more hours."

"Yes," she said, and sat down on the sofa. "Did you talk to the limo driver?"

"Yeah. Riley paid him an extra hundred to keep his wheelchair ready for the return ride and not to talk to anyone about it."

"How much did it cost you?"

Jim grinned. "Just a threat or two. You know, accessory to a felony. He already has a record. He didn't want to be sent back to jail."

"How fortunate," she said with a smile.

An awkward silence fell. Finally Jim said, "How about dinner? It's a little early, but we'll avoid the crowds. Then we can go to another show tonight. Maybe the Celine Dion show."

"That's a strange choice for a guy," Carrie said, distracted by his choice.

"Would you rather I suggest a burlesque show?" he asked, wiggling his eyebrows. "Actually, I was just trying to think of a show that you would enjoy."

"I think I know one that we'd both enjoy if we can get tickets."

"What's that?"

"George Strait. He's performing at one of the hotels."

"Perfect, Carrie. Good thinking. I'll go see if I can get tickets."

"All right."

Half an hour later, Jim returned with two tickets. Their excitement carried them through dinner, and the show was as terrific as they'd anticipated. When Jim caught Carrie's hand as they walked back to the Bellagio, she didn't even protest.

She tensed up when they entered their suite, however.

Jim could see the difference. He'd enjoyed their evening together, sharing an interest, going on an actual date for the first time. "What's wrong?"

She tugged her hand from his and turned away. "Nothing. I guess I'm tired."

Since they had gone to the early show and it was now only a little after ten, he didn't really believe that. "Want me to take the sofa tonight?"

"No. I like to watch late-night television."

"Because you're so tired? Be honest with me, Carrie."

"Fine! I don't like sharing a room with you. It—it makes me nervous!"

"You don't trust me?" he asked softly.

"Of course I do!"

"Now that doesn't make sense, either. If you trust me not to do anything you don't want me to do, then what's the problem?"

Carrie backed toward the wall, as if she was being cornered. After licking her lips, which got Jim's attention, she said quietly, "I don't trust myself."

Jim took a step closer. "What are you talking about?"

"Just go in the other room and leave me alone," she insisted.

"I don't think so," he said, moving closer. "I think I might like what you might like. I've been struggling to hold back all the time we've been here. Tonight…well, it was our first date. Did you realize that?"

"No, we had dinner together several times."

"Those were pity dates," Jim said ruefully.

She jerked her head up, anger in her eyes. "I don't need any pity dates!"

"Not you, sweetheart. Me. Those were pity dates for me. You felt sorry for me being so lonely, so you agreed to go out with me. I knew what they were, but I wanted to spend time with you. So I took what you offered."

"You—you wanted to spend time with me?" Carrie asked, her voice wavering.

"Yeah. I thought you'd figured that out."

"No. When you winked for me to rescue you, you… you didn't really need rescuing?"

Jim grinned. "Now that encouraged me. You thought you had to protect *me*. I figured I was giving the marines a bad name."

"I know you could handle yourself in a fight, but you certainly couldn't go one on one with Stella like you did with Trevor."

"Stella wouldn't have objected," he teased.

Carrie reached out and slapped his arm. "You're being very bad."

"Naw, honey, I've been very, very good. But I'd like to be better…with you. I'm going out of my mind wondering if you want a friend…or a lover."

When she kept her gaze down and didn't answer, he hurriedly said, "It's all right, Carrie. I know it's too soon for you to have figured that out. But when you're ready, just let me know," he said, his voice taut with frustration.

Carrie lifted her blue gaze to his face and said softly, "I'm ready."

"You're ready to let me know?" he asked, frowning.

"No, I'm ready to be your lover," she said firmly, leaving no doubt.

He stared at her. "Are you sure?"

"What's the matter? Do you think the marines are the only ones who can make up their minds?" she teased. "I fell for you long before I met you."

"Because of my picture?" he asked.

"You know about that?" She looked horrified.

"I saw it on your desk the first time I came to the office. It's all right, I understand that's how you work." His words seemed to soothe her because her expression relaxed.

"The more I learned about you, though," she admitted, "the more I fell for you. You're a complicated man. Able to do the hard things that most people can't do. Yet you have such love and caring in you, beyond anyone's definition of love, I would be honored to be your friend." She paused. "But I would prefer to love you in every way possible."

Carrie knew marines were men of action. Jim proved it by scooping her up in his arms and carrying her to bed. Every step of the way he kissed her, the deep kisses she'd dreamed about for so long. The kisses she'd thought would never happen in real life.

By the time he slid her down his body in the bedroom, she'd begun to undo the buttons on his shirt. She wanted to see that massive chest she'd only glimpsed earlier. As the shirt came off, she stroked him, feeling his muscles, hard and firm, knowing he had the strength to protect her if she needed it.

Jim had been doing his own exploration, releasing her bra with an expertise that had her wondering about his past.

Then they separated to remove the rest of the bothersome clothes before they fell to the mattress, reaching for each other. After several minutes of touching, kissing, stroking, Carrie pulled back. "Jim, I should—"

"Don't worry, honey. A good marine is always prepared." He found his pants and pulled out a condom. Then he rejoined Carrie, pulling her back into his arms.

She'd intended to warn him, but that warning was unnecessary a few minutes later when he tried to enter her. She tensed, but her words and body urged him to make them one. As he did, he looked at her. "You were a virgin?" he demanded, surprise and concern mingling in his voice.

"Am I not doing it right?" she cried out, eager to have him continue.

He attempted to pull out, but she pleaded with him not to go. With a sigh, he pushed farther and began a rocking movement, his arms around her, his kisses making her more eager than ever. They both experienced completion at the same time.

Carrie clung to Jim, wanting to say so many things, but she couldn't get anything out. A boneless lassitude came over her and she curled up against him. As she drifted off to sleep, she held on to him, thanking her stars that the real thing was better than any fantasy.

JIM WATCHED the woman asleep in his arms. He couldn't believe this was her first time with a man. Nor could he help rejoicing that he was her first. And he had every intention of being her last. In the morning they'd talk and maybe make love again.

The thought of always having Carrie beside him was wonderful.

Tomorrow he'd buy her a ring, he told himself as he fell asleep. Everything would work out tomorrow.

But tomorrow dawned quite differently than what he'd expected.

He woke slowly and kissed the top of Carrie's head, which was once again resting on his shoulder, thinking that he'd slept better than he could ever remember. But then his eyes lit on the clock on the nightstand—7:15 a.m. The time pierced his brain like a sharp sword. Their flight left in forty-five minutes.

"Carrie!" His cry roused her immediately. "We've got to get to the airport. Hurry."

He jumped out of bed and began searching the floor for the clothing he'd haphazardly discarded the night before. As he did, he glanced up at Carrie, who sat there with the sheet up to her neck. "We've got to hurry. Just slip into your clothes from last night. I'll help you pack."

His sense of urgency penetrated her head and she did as he said, even though she longed for a shower. They were dressed in five minutes, took another five to pack, then they hurried to the lobby to pay their bill.

"The airport is only ten minutes away, sir," the clerk said as she waved to one of the bellboys. "Go get a cab ready for Mr. and Mrs. Barlow, please."

They got to the airport fifteen minutes before their flight was to leave. Sympathetic passengers let them go ahead of them in the security line. Then they ran down the hallway to the gate.

"You just barely made it," the attendant said in a sharp voice. "We're ready to push away from the gate."

"We overslept," Jim said with a smile that eased the severity of her frown.

Once they were on the plane, Carrie snapped on her seat belt and then thought about what had happened. They'd made love last night. At least it had been love on her part. She couldn't remember Jim saying that he loved her. Or talking about the future.

Maybe he'd been so horrified to find out she was inexperienced, he had no interest in the future. Should she promise to get better? No, that would sound too much like begging. Besides, she refused to discuss her private life on an airplane. She immediately closed her eyes, determined to pretend to sleep all the way back to Dallas.

Somewhere within two minutes she stopped pretending and actually fell asleep.

Jim got a pillow from the stewardess and propped it behind Carrie's head against the window. Then he spent a lot of time just staring at her. He'd promised himself they'd talk this morning, but oversleeping had ruined his plans.

Once they were home they'd talk.

A little over two hours later, the plane landed in Dallas. Carrie still slept. After the passengers around them had filed out, he woke her. "Carrie, we're in Dallas. Come on, honey, let's go home."

She opened her eyes and began to gather her purse, then her overhead luggage, to exit the plane. Jim followed her, eager to get her home, where they could be alone.

As they came out of the airport, Will called to them.

"What are you doing here, Will?" Jim asked, frowning.

"We're having a Sunday family luncheon to celebrate your success. We can't wait to tomorrow to hear the details. Carrie, come ride with me so you can tell me all about it."

Carrie agreed, without looking at Jim.

The two of them walked off, leaving Jim standing there alone.

He drove as fast as he could and it looked like he got there first, because Will's car wasn't there. Rushing into the house, he said, "I got here before Will and Carrie, I guess. I'm sure they'll be here any minute," he said to Vanessa, who'd let him in.

"Actually, no. He took Carrie to her apartment so she could take a shower and change clothes. They'll be here in about half an hour."

Jim stared at her, a crazed look in his eyes.

"Is something wrong?" Vanessa asked.

"Yes! No! I don't know!"

"Jim, what's wrong?"

He stared at her blankly. Then he suddenly said, "I need to talk to you."

"Well, of course. Rebecca and Jeff and the kids are here. We're visiting in the—"

"No! I mean, maybe Rebecca, but I can't— This is private!"

"Go to the library and I'll go get Rebecca. We'll both come help you."

After asking Rebecca to come with her to the kitchen, she redirected her older sister into the library. "Jim is behaving very strangely."

The two young women came in to the library to find their brother pacing back and forth.

"Jim, what's wrong?" Rebecca asked.

"I—I think I did something wrong."

"What?" Vanessa demanded. She was becoming a little impatient with her brother.

"Carrie and I made love last night."

Vanessa squealed and clapped her hands together. "How wonderful."

Jim glared at her. "Is it?"

"Isn't it?" Rebecca asked.

"I don't know. We talked about being lovers but— but I don't think I told her I love her. Do you think she understood?"

"Did you talk at all?" Rebecca asked.

"Yeah. I left the decision up to her. I thought she wasn't ready yet but she said she was."

"Then what's the problem?" Vanessa asked.

Jim started pacing again.

"You're driving us crazy, Jim," Vanessa said. "Just tell us what the problem is."

"It was her first time," he muttered.

Total silence followed his words.

"Oh, my," Vanessa said with a sigh. "Did you talk after?"

"No. She fell asleep almost at once. I told myself we'd talk this morning."

"And did you?" Rebecca asked, a little bit of sternness in her voice.

"I couldn't. We overslept and almost didn't catch our plane."

"What are you going to do?" Vanessa asked.

"I don't know. I told myself we'd talk when we got back to the apartments, but then Will met us at the airport and kidnapped her. I don't know what to do."

"It's possible she may not come to lunch. It's even possible she'll resign her job," Rebecca said.

"No! She can't. I won't allow her to do that!"

"Jim," Rebecca said quietly, "who told you you were in control?"

"I did. I'm going over to the apartments. Call Will and tell him I'm coming, that I have to have a few minutes with Carrie alone."

He was out the door before either sister could say anything.

WILL OPENED the door to Carrie's apartment when Jim knocked softly. "I'm glad you're here," he said. "What's going on?"

"Did she say something?"

"Only that she was quitting. What happened in Vegas?"

"She's not resigning. It's a misunderstanding, that's all. Let me talk to her alone. Then we'll come to lunch."

"Are you sure? I told her I wouldn't accept her resignation, and she started crying."

Jim heard the pain in Will's voice. "I promise you Will. If anyone leaves, it will be me, not Carrie. But I hope I can convince her to let both of us stay."

"All right. I'll trust you to do what's best for Carrie," Will said, though there was a hint of a question in his words.

Jim didn't dare try to explain to Will because the older man might slug him. But Carrie had agreed that it was what she wanted. He just wasn't sure she still felt that way.

"I'll let you know as soon as I can."

After Will left, he sat down on the sofa and waited, though he would've preferred to join Carrie in the shower. He promised himself he'd do that one day, but they had to talk before they did anything like that again.

A few minutes later Carrie stepped into the living room, her hair blown dry, and wearing a pair of pants and sweater. She moved into the kitchen and put on water for hot tea.

"Are you all right?"

She whipped around, spilling water out of the kettle. "Oh! You—you scared me."

He stood and walked into the kitchen. Gently he asked, "Did I scare you last night?"

"No, I wasn't scared last night."

The words should've pleased him, but she dropped her gaze.

"Then why won't you look at me?"

"I think you'd better go to Will and Vivian's for lunch. They're waiting on you."

"Aren't you going?"

"No."

"Why not?"

She squared her shoulders and drew a deep breath. "Because I'm leaving the firm. It would be too awkward for us."

"I won't allow it!"

"It's not your decision!" she protested.

He stepped closer. "Why would you do such a thing?"

She turned her back. "I made a mistake."

"What mistake?"

There was a longer silence this time, and she didn't turn around to face him. But he waited her out.

"I—I thought I could be your lover and it wouldn't change anything. But I was wrong."

"Did Will convince you of that?"

"No. We didn't discuss my reasons."

"Good. Because I'm pretty sure you're wrong. You see, you fell asleep last night before we could talk. And this morning we overslept and didn't have time. But I don't think I can work with you and Will *without* my being your lover." He reached for her shoulders and gently turned her around to face him. With his thumb he caught one of the tears rolling down her face. "You see, I want to be your husband as well as your lover."

If he'd thought she would immediately be transported into ecstasy, he was mistaken.

"That's not necessary!"

He frowned. "I'm missing something here. Ah, I forgot to say the three little words I should've said last night. But I got distracted. I love you, Carrie."

Still no happiness. The tears started coming much faster than before.

She shook her head, sobbing, while she tried to answer him.

Taking a tissue from the counter, he started mopping up her cheeks. "Wait until you stop crying, honey, 'cause I can't understand you right now."

"I said you d-don't have to say that."

The sadness in her voice almost broke his heart. "Yes, I do, because it's the truth. I thought you understood last night that I love you, but I guess I should've spelled it out."

"But you don't now!"

"Why don't I?"

"Be—because I was…inexperienced!"

He cradled her against him. "I wish I could say there was no one before you, but it's not true. But I wish it was. Making love to you was the sweetest thing I've ever done. However, if I'd known before, I would've waited until our wedding night. At least I hope I would've."

"R-really?" she asked, hiccupping.

"Really. I love you with all my heart. I hesitated in the beginning because I thought I was a jinx."

"I know. Vanessa told me."

"Ah. My little sister has been busy. But I'll forgive her since she tried to set us up at her party."

"No, she wanted you to meet someone—"

"And I did. I met you, again. And held you in my arms. And kissed you."

"But you regretted it."

"No, I just made up an excuse. That kiss stayed on

my mind for several days, until we got to Vegas and I got to kiss you again."

He leaned in and was about to kiss her when the phone rang.

"I bet that's Will. We're going to have to go over there, you know, even though I'd prefer to go to bed." He moved to the phone and answered it.

"Well? Have you convinced her?" Will asked him.

Jim turned to Carrie and said, "Will wants to know if I convinced you. What shall I tell him?"

"Tell him yes and we're on our way," she said, smiling.

"Yeah," he said into the phone. He listened for a moment. "Yeah, in a couple of minutes."

When he turned around and took her in his arms, she asked, "Didn't you tell Will we were on our way?"

"Yep. And we are. Just as soon as I kiss you again."

She had no objections to those plans.

Welcome to the world of American Romance!
Turn the page for excerpts from our
August 2005 titles.

A FABULOUS WIFE by Dianne Castell

JUDGING JOSHUA by Mary Anne Wilson

HOMEWARD BOUND by Marin Thomas

THE ULTIMATE TEXAS BACHELOR
by Cathy Gillen Thacker

We're sure you'll enjoy every one
of these books!

A FABULOUS WIFE
by Dianne Castell

A FABULOUS WIFE *is the first of three hu-
morous books about three women in Whistlers
Bend, Montana, who are turning forty and how
they're dealing—or not dealing—with it. You'll
love this new miniseries from Dianne Castell,
called* FORTY & FABULOUS.

Watch for A FABULOUS HUSBAND,
coming in October.

Sweat beaded across Jack Dawson's forehead. His stomach clenched. The red LCD numbers on the timer clocked backward. Thirty seconds to make up his mind before this son of a bitch blew sky-high...taking the First National Bank of Chicago and him along for the ride.

What the hell was he doing here? Forty-one was too old for this. He was a detective, a hostage negotiator, not a damn bomb expert...except when the bomb squad got caught in gridlock on Michigan Avenue and the hostage was an uptown financial institution.

He thought of his son graduating...by the sheer grace of a benevolent God...next week in Whistlers Bend, Montana. He couldn't miss that. Maggie would be there, of course. Had it really been ten years since he'd seen his ex? She hated his being a cop. *At the moment he wasn't too thrilled about it, either.*

He remembered Maggie's blue eyes. Maybe it *was* time for a change.

Always cut white? He held his breath, muttered a prayer, zeroed in on the blue wire...and cut.

JUDGING JOSHUA
by Mary Anne Wilson

In Mary Anne Wilson's four-book series
RETURN TO SILVER CREEK,
*various characters return to a small Nevada
town for a variety of reasons—to hide, to come
home, to confront their pasts. In this second
book, police officer Joshua Pierce finds himself
back in the hometown he was desperate to
escape—and is now unable to leave.*

Going back to Silver Creek, Nevada, should have been a good thing. But going home was hard on Joshua Pierce.

He stepped out of the old stone-and-brick police station and into the bitter cold of November. The brilliance of the sun glinting off the last snowfall made him narrow his eyes as he shrugged into his heavy green uniform jacket. Even though he was only wearing a white T-shirt underneath, Joshua didn't bother doing it up as he headed for the closest squad car in the security parking lot to the side of the station.

Easing his six-foot frame into the cruiser, he turned on the motor and flipped the heater on high, waiting for warmth. Two months ago he'd been in the humid heat of an Atlanta September, without any thoughts of coming home. Then his world shifted, the way it had over a year ago, but this time it was his father who needed him.

He pushed the car into gear, hit the release for the security gate, then drove out onto the side street. He was back in Silver Creek without any idea what he'd do when he left here again. And he *would* leave. After all, this wasn't home anymore. For now he was filling in for his father, taking life day by day. It worked. He made it to the next day, time and time again. And that was enough for him, for now.

He turned north on the main street, through the center of a valley framed by the rugged peaks of the Sierra Nevadas soaring into the heavy gray sky to the west and east. Here, some of the best skiing in the west had been a guarded secret for years. Then the word got out, and Silver Creek joined the skiing boom.

The old section of town looked about the same, with stone-and-brick buildings, some dating back to the silver strike in the 1800s. Though on the surface this area seemed like a relic from the past, if you looked more closely, the feed store was now a high-end ski-equipment shop and the general store had been transformed into a trendy coffee bar and specialty cookie store.

Some buildings were the same, such as Rusty's Diner and the Silver Creek Hotel. But everything was changing—even in Silver Creek, change was inevitable. You couldn't fight it, he thought as he drove farther north, into the newer section of town where the stores were unabashedly expensive. He'd tried to fight the changes in his life—all his life—but in the end, he hadn't been able to change a thing. Which is why he was now back in Silver Creek and would be leaving again, sooner or later.

He could only hope it would be sooner.

HOMEWARD BOUND
by Marin Thomas

*Marin Thomas hails from the Dairy State—
Wisconsin—but Texas is now home. It's a good
thing, because there is never a shortage of cowboys—and never a shortage of interesting men to
write about, as* HOMEWARD BOUND *shows!*

"Just like old times, huh, Heather?"

The beer bottle halfway to Heather Henderson's mouth froze. Her heart thumped wildly and her muscles bunched, preparing her body for flight. If the voice belonged to whom she assumed, then she was in big trouble.

Longingly, she eyed the bottle in her hand—her first alcoholic drink in over two months, and she hadn't even gotten to take a sip—then lowered it and wiggled it against her Hawaiian skirt. After sucking in a deep breath, she slowly turned and faced her past.

Oh, my.

At six feet two inches, minus the black Stetson, the mayor of Nowhere, Texas, didn't exactly blend in with the gaggle of bikini-clad college coeds in her dorm celebrating end-of-year finals—luau-style. Even if he exchanged his western shirt, Wranglers and tattered cowboy boots for a pair of swim trunks, he wouldn't fit in—not with his stony face and grim personality. "Hello, Royce. Your timing is impeccable…as usual."

Eyes dark as chunks of coal stared solemnly at her

from under the brim of his seen-better-days cowboy hat. His eyes shifted to the bottle peeking out from under her costume, and his mouth twisted into a cynical frown. "Some people never change…. Still the party queen, Heather?"

Obviously he believed she'd held a bottle of beer in her hand more than a textbook since enrolling in college four years ago. She hated the way he always assumed the worst of people. Then again, maybe he was right—some people never changed. *He* appeared to be the same brooding, arrogant know-it-all she remembered from her teen years.

"I'm almost twenty-three." She lifted her chin. "Last time I checked, the legal drinking age in Texas was twenty-one."

His gaze roamed the lobby. "I suppose all these students are twenty-one?"

Rolling her eyes, she snapped, "I see you haven't gotten rid of that trusty soapbox of yours."

The muscle along his jaw ticked and anger sparkled in his eyes—a sure sign he was gearing up for an argument. She waited for her body to tense and her stomach to twist into a knot, but surprisingly, a tingle skittered down her spine instead, leaving her breathless and perplexed.

Shaking off the weird feeling, she set her hands on her hips. "So what if we're breaking the no-alcohol-in-the-dorm rule? No one's in danger of getting written up."

"Just how do you figure that?" he asked.

THE ULTIMATE TEXAS BACHELOR
by *Cathy Gillen Thacker*

*Welcome back to Laramie, Texas, and
a whole new crop of cowboys!
Cathy Gillen Thacker's new series*
THE McCABES: NEXT GENERATION
*evolved from her popular American Romance
series* **THE McCABES OF TEXAS.**
*Read this first book of the three,
and find out why this author is a favorite among
American Romance readers!*

"Come on, Lainey. Have a heart! You can't leave us like this!" Lewis McCabe declared as he pushed his eyeglasses farther up on the bridge of his nose.

Besides the fact she was here under false pretenses—which she had quickly decided she couldn't go through with, anyway—Lainey Carrington didn't see how she could stay, either. The Lazy M ranch house looked like a college dorm room had exploded on moving day. Lewis needed a lot more than the live-in housekeeper he had been advertising for to bring order to this mess.

"What do you mean *us?*" she asked suspiciously. Was Lewis married? If so, she hadn't heard about it, but then she hadn't actually lived in Laramie, Texas, since she had left home for college ten years before.

The door behind Lainey opened. She turned and darn near fainted at the sight of the man she had secretly come here to track down.

Not that she had expected the six-foot-three cowboy with the ruggedly handsome face and to-die-for body to actually be here. She had just hoped that Lewis would give her a clue where to look so that she might help her friend Sybil Devine hunt down the elusive Brad McCabe and scrutinize the sexy Casanova celebrity in person. "Brad, of course, who happens to be my business partner," Lewis McCabe explained.

"Actually, I'm more of a ranch manager," Brad McCabe corrected grimly, shooting an aggravated look at his younger brother. He knocked some of the mud off his scuffed brown leather boots, then stepped into the interior of the sprawling half-century-old ranch house. "And I thought we had an agreement, Lewis, that you'd let me know when we were going to have company so I could avoid running into 'em."

Lewis shot Lainey an apologetic glance. "Don't mind him. He's been in a bad mood ever since he got done filming that reality TV show."

Lainey took this opportunity to gather a little background research. "Guess it didn't exactly have the happily-ever-after ending everyone expected it to have," she observed.

Brad's jaw set. Clearly he did not want her sympathy. "You saw it?"

Obviously he wished she hadn't. Lainey shrugged, not about to admit just how riveted she'd been by the sight of Brad McCabe on her television screen. "I think everyone who knows you did."

"Not to mention most of America," Lewis chimed in.

Bachelor Bliss had pulled in very high ratings, especially at the end, when it had taken an unexpected twist. The success wasn't surprising, given how sexy Brad had looked walking out of the ocean in only a pair of swim trunks that had left very little to the imagination when wet.

"You shouldn't have wasted your time watching such bull," Brad muttered, scowl deepening as his voice dropped a self-deprecating notch. "And I know I shouldn't have wasted mine filming it."

Lainey agreed with him wholeheartedly there. Going on an artificially romantic TV show was no way to find a mate. "For what it's worth, I don't think they did right by you," Lainey continued.

She had heard from mutual acquaintances that Brad McCabe's experience as the sought-after bachelor on *Bachelor Bliss* had turned him into not just a persona non grata where the entire viewing public was concerned, but also into a hardened cynic. That assumption seemed to be true, judging by the scowl on his face and the unwelcoming light in his eyes as he swept off his straw cowboy hat and ran his fingers through his gleaming dark brown hair.

If you enjoyed what you just read,
then we've got an offer you can't resist!

Take 2 bestselling love stories FREE!

Plus get a FREE surprise gift!